NURSE

'A dream of a doctor'—that was what all
the nursing staff of Highcastle Hospital in
Northumbria called Adam Sheridan. All,
that is, except Staff Nurse Isobel Ford,
who resented the coldly handsome Dr
Sheridan's jibes about her Southern
origins.

NURSE ISOBEL'S DREAM

BY
HAZEL FISHER

MILLS & BOON LIMITED
15–16 BROOK'S MEWS
LONDON W1A 1DR

First published in Great Britain 1985 by Mills & Boon Limited

© Hazel Fisher 1985

Australian copyright 1985 Philippine copyright 1985

ISBN 0 263 75265 8

Set in 11 on 12 pt Linotron Times
03–1285–46,200

Photoset by Rowland Phototypesetting Limited Bury St Edmunds, Suffolk Made and printed in Great Britain by Richard Clay (The Chaucer Press) Limited Bungay, Suffolk

CHAPTER ONE

IT was June again already—a hot, sultry June following a cold, wet May. Isobel Ford was uncomfortable in the thick blue staff nurse's uniform and longed for the cool white dresses she had worn at the London hospital where she had trained. But London was many miles away from Highcastle General Hospital, which was set on the outskirts of the market town of Highcastle in the Northumbrian countryside.

She rose from her seat behind Sister Sowerby's desk, a slightly-built, graceful figure, the staff nurse's lacy cap set atop her short reddish-brown curls. Sister was on leave and Isobel was temporarily in charge of Bladen Ward, women's medical. She cast a practised eye over the ward, which was arranged on Victorian lines, a long row of beds down each side plus three small, glass-panelled side rooms just the other side of the clinic.

All seemed peaceful, and she settled back to read Mrs Chipchase's notes again. Muriel Chipchase was a patient in her late fifties suffering from advanced multiple sclerosis, and Isobel had grown fond of her. In fact she was fond of all her patients, even those few who grumbled incessantly.

The end of June would mark her first anniversary on the ward, the end of her first year at the hospital, come to that. She had arrived, a heartbroken newly qualified nurse; now, at twenty-three, she was an experienced and mature staff nurse. Despite the heartache which had brought her so many miles from London, the year had been a reasonably happy one. The only fly in the ointment on Bladen was Dr Adam Sheridan, the senior consultant—a 'dream of a doctor', as the nursing staff called him. All the nursing staff, that was, except Isobel; she kept out of his way whenever possible. With Sister away this week that would not be possible, though, and an involuntary tremor shot through her slender body, half fear, half anticipation—pleasurable anticipation. If Adam Sheridan was a hateful, fault-finding pain in the neck he was also an exceedingly charismatic man, and Isobel wasn't immune to his attractions, despite her resolve never to become involved with a man again. The savage emotional wound Dr Paul Ashe had inflicted a year ago was still raw, unhealed, and it would take more than the coldly handsome Adam Sheridan to . . .

'Daydreaming, Staff? Is that all you south country people do?'

Isobel started guiltily, then smiled as Dr David Hanington settled his long, gangling body in the chair opposite. He was Dr Sheridan's registrar and Isobel liked him a lot. He and his wife, Lynne, had done much to ease her transition to a different world, a different culture. They were Geordie through and through, with a warm, open friendli-ness Isobel found hard to resist after the anonymity and starkness of London life.

Without Paul's love, everywhere had seemed stark and unfriendly at first, she acknowledged. Yet somehow she had survived and would go on surviving, despite his parting shot, an almost mortal blow.

Her green eyes darkened with the still vividly remembered hurt, the shock, and David leaned forward, his eyes concerned. 'Are you in pain, Isobel? Your face changed, then.'

She summoned up a smile. 'I hope it was a change for the better!' she quipped, rising to glance down the ward again. Of course Bladen wasn't unattended. State-Enrolled Nurse Mackenzie was at the other end talking to a patient and their first-year student, Aimee Ruddock, was just about to start another bedpan round with one of the auxiliaries. Isobel frowned. The third-year ought to be there keeping an eye on Aimee, who had only been on the ward a couple of weeks . . .

'Busy, Staff Nurse?'

David Hanington sprang up and almost stood to attention, and Isobel turned warily to face the tall, dark-haired, commanding figure of Dr Adam Sheridan. He stood just inside the door, chilly grey eyes surveying what must have seemed to him a cosy domestic scene.

A small sigh escaped Isobel, and the consultant raised a dark brow, without speaking. He never *needed* to speak. He could convey a message by the merest gesture, and the message he was conveying to Isobel was unmistakable. She was a lazy southerner and it was a pity she had ever made the trip north. A pity she had landed on *his* ward, at any rate.

Smouldering with anger without showing it was a trick she had learned since meeting Dr Sheridan, and her gaze was cool but not unfriendly as she greeted him. Consultants had to be addressed correctly and politely, no matter how arrogant and chauvinistic they were. And Dr Sheridan was a chauvinist with a capital 'C'!

'Good afternoon, sir.' She forced a smile and hoped it didn't look as unnatural as it felt. 'I'm afraid Sister is on leave this week and I . . .'

'*That* much is obvious,' he cut in, advancing towards her. For one awful moment she thought he was about to strike her and she flinched, unable to stop the involuntary gesture.

He stopped just short of the desk, however, and gazed down at her, dark grey eyes watchful. 'Let me see Mrs Chipchase's notes, will you,' he commanded, the deep masculine voice doing strange, exciting things to her nerve ends. despite the intense dislike she felt for the man.

'I was just reading them, sir,' she told him, wondering if there had been some new development. In Mrs Chipchase's case any new developments would be minus ones. The woman was on the ward only because there was nowhere else for her to go. She was awaiting a place in a Cheshire Home, but such vacancies were rare and she had been on Bladen three weeks already. If death did not supervene she might still be with them three months hence.

'Why were you reading them? Do you have a particular interest in MS patients?' the consultant queried, settling himself on the edge of Sister's desk. David, she noted with annoyance, had made a silent escape, leaving her to cope with his chief.

She shook her head, aware that he would not be interested in her answer. Her reasons were private, anyway. The movement of her head caused the lace cap to slip and it ended up perched just above her right ear. She remembered too late that she was one grip short and that the cap wasn't as secure as usual. His frosty gaze followed the gesture, though he didn't comment, dropping his eyes again to the notes. Isobel blushed, her face going as red as her hair, thankful that he couldn't see it. He would know, of course; he never missed a thing.

It would be nice, she thought wistfully, if they could be friends, or at least friendly enough for her to question him about Mrs Chipchase and the disease which had brought her to the hospital. The general medical consultant at her London hospital had always listened to her, answered her questions with a grave courtesy that . . .

'Are you with me, Nurse Ford?' He was watching her now and she wished she was back home, many, many miles from Bladen Ward *and* from Dr Sheridan!

'Yes, sir,' she said crisply. 'Is there a vacancy yet for Mrs Chipchase?'

'No! They don't grow on trees, Staff Nurse.' His tone was sharp, and Isobel felt aggrieved. She had a right to ask, surely? She glanced out of the big window again, noting the progress of the bedpan trolley. She . . .

'Fetch me Mrs Elliott's notes,' he commanded, and Isobel's eyes flashed fire at him before she could control herself.

What might have been amusement touched his strong face and hastily she averted her gaze. He was too attractive by far. Each feature was indelibly printed upon her memory. The sensuous mouth, the straight nose, determined chin with just the hint of a cleft in its centre, those chilly, watchful eyes . . .

The phone shrilled, jerking her wayward thoughts back to the present, the cold reality of being in charge of a ward where the consultant despised her. It was Reception, asking if Dr Sheridan was there. 'Yes, he's here. Did you want to speak to him or—'

'No, no, dear.' The receptionist's cheery voice could be heard clearly by the doctor and he lifted his eyes from the notes, his expression alert. 'It's just a message. There's a Miss Kenlow down in Reception—says Dr Sheridan is expecting her, and should she wait here?'

Isobel turned enquiring eyes on the doctor, who nodded. 'Say I'll be down to see my fiancée in a few minutes.'

She repeated the message, a coldness creeping through her body. Miss Kenlow was his fiancée. Dr Sheridan was engaged to be married!

She was about to make some excuse about supervising the bedpan round, but there was no need. Without another word the consultant handed back Mrs Elliott's notes and strode from the room, his long legs soon carrying him from her sight. Shaken and disturbed both by his visit and by the news of a fiancée, Isobel made her way slowly down the ward. It was time she spoke to Mrs Chipchase, something she tried to do whenever she had a few minutes to spare.

Muriel Chipchase's sad brown eyes lit up as Isobel entered the glass-partitioned side room. From the room Mrs Chipchase could see and be seen, but she still felt isolated and alone. The decubitus ulcers weren't healing very well and added to her distress. They were the result of being nursed inadequately at home by her elder sister and could not have been prevented without expert care. The staff on Bladen Ward had kept the ulcers under control and some had healed, but the patient's skin was now so delicate and had such a poor blood supply that it was a difficult task.

'There's no news of a vacancy yet, Mrs Chipchase,' Isobel said gently, squeezing the woman's hand and settling herself by the bed. From where she sat she could still keep a covert eye on the ward and the staff could see her if anything untoward happened. Only a week or two before, a patient had suffered a massive coronary there and had died on the way to ITU, so even in a medical ward it wasn't always plain sailing.

'Dr Sheridan did say he had something in view,' Mrs Chipchase ventured, and Isobel's eyes widened in surprise.

'Did he? That must be why . . .' she began, then stopped, but Mrs Chipchase insisted she finish the sentence. 'Doctor was looking at your notes,' Isobel went on reluctantly, aware that she shouldn't be telling the woman. 'I asked him if there was a place for you yet and he said no. He didn't mention a vacancy anywhere else. He's probably making further enquiries and didn't want to say until he was sure. I expect something will turn up soon.'

The words of comfort rolled glibly off her lips and she hoped the patient believed her. Places for the younger chronically ill and disabled were scarce, and she wondered why Dr Sheridan had even mentioned a possible vacancy. It was wicked to raise her hopes in that way. In any case, Mrs Chipchase was comfortable enough on Bladen even though she was so helpless. Lifting was a problem as she was a heavy woman, though losing weight now.

She left Mrs Chipchase and went over to their young diabetic patient, Christine Hemsley. Chris was a live-wire and always eased the cares of the nursing staff. On admission she had been near death. She was excitable and didn't always stick to her diet or remember to inject her insulin at the proper times. She was now stabilised again, but it was the second time in a year that Isobel had seen her and no doubt it would not be the last.

'Ready for the off, Chris?' she asked brightly, and Chris nodded enthusiastically.

'Can't wait to get home! My boy-friend is picking me up straight after breakfast tomorrow.' She put her head on one side and eyed Isobel speculatively. 'Have you got a boy-friend, Staff Nurse? I hear there's a party in the Nurses' Home tomorrow night and I'd like to think of you enjoying yourself.'

Isobel felt that familiar stab of pain again. 'I did have a boy-friend,' she admitted slowly, wondering why the pain was still so deep, so intense, even after a year. 'But that was in London. He's a long way from the wild north!' she smiled, masking her aching heart. Patients were not interested in a nurse's heartache, her problems. True, they *were* interested in nurses' romantic lives, often pairing a Sister or staff nurse off with a consultant quite unsuitably. There was talk about Sister Sowerby, an attractive blonde widow, and Adam Sheridan. *That* would soon be scotched now. Once the receptionist spread the news of a fiancée the whole hospital would be buzzing.

'Is anything the matter, Staff Nurse?' Chris's gaze was shrewd and Isobel coloured faintly. 'Worried about your boy-friend, are you? You must miss him.'

'No, not at all,' Isobel denied firmly, hoping Chris wouldn't see through the lie. 'I was thinking about Mrs Chipchase, actually. I wish I could offer her more comfort. Do you suppose you could pop in to see her before you go?' she went on. 'I know it's hard seeing her suffer, but she gets terribly lonely, and I know she enjoys the company of young people.'

To her relief, the girl nodded, fair curls dancing. 'Of course I will. If you think that's what she would want,' she went on doubtfully.

Having reassured Chris and promised to bring in some magazines she could give to Mrs Chipchase, Isobel moved on. It was a big ward, thirty beds plus the three side rooms, and by the time she had finished her round and seen that all the nursing duties were carried out, it was supper time, visiting time, then the hand-over to the night staff nurse.

Isobel said good night to all those patients who were still awake, but when she peered in at Mrs Chipchase the woman was sleeping. Satisfied that all was as it should be, she left in the company of SEN Joy Mackenzie, a small plump and cheerful Geordie.

'I see our dream of a doctor was in the office with you!' Joy chuckled, and Isobel didn't know what to say in reply. She made a noncommittal noise and nodded, which seemed to satisfy Joy. 'He's a lovely lad. Wish he'd glance *my* way,' the bubbly SEN went on, and Isobel smiled wanly.

'He doesn't glance *my* way, if that's what you're thinking.' She hesitated, wondering if she should mention the mysterious Miss Kenlow, then decided against it. The other nurses would hear soon enough without her gossiping about their senior doctor's private life. 'He was looking at Mrs Chipchase's notes, but I don't know why,' she said instead, and Joy nodded.

'That's because she's multiple sclerosis. He has a special interest in the disease, apparently.'

'Oh? Why? It comes under the neurology speciality. He's general.'

'Why, aye, I know that, but he's keen for some reason.'

They parted company, Joy Mackenzie leaving by the side entrance which led to the car-park, Isobel walking the short distance to the Nurses' Home where, until recently, she had shared a flat with another staff nurse, her friend Sadie Philips. She had no other home now, not even in London, and no family either, her parents having been killed in an air crash soon after she had started her nurse training.

She and Sadie had trained together, and when Sadie announced her intention of returning to Northumberland to nurse, Isobel had joined her. She needed to get away from everything that reminded her of Paul Ashe, and she was glad of Sadie's company. Then, after a whirlwind courtship, Sadie had married last Christmas and was now working abroad with her doctor husband. So Isobel was alone again. No Sadie and no Paul Ashe.

Once inside the flat the loneliness closed in on her and she hurriedly switched on the radio. The bombshell that Adam Sheridan had dropped about having a fiancée made her restless and uneasy. It surely could not be that she was falling for the man!

She lay in bed later, far from sleep. She was on early duty in the morning—Adam's round day. Her pulses quickened. She would see him again tomorrow! It was ridiculous. She hated men. She would always have to keep them at a distance anyway, for hadn't Paul told her what she was?

'You're a frigid, abnormal girl'. The words echoed from the past and she wanted to lash out at him with her tongue. Just because she hadn't wanted to sleep with him he'd called her frigid. It was simply hurt male pride, nothing more.

Isobel bit her lip savagely, feeling again the pain of his words, the pain of rejection, too. 'I'm not frigid. I'm *not*,' she whispered into the darkness. The attraction she felt for Adam Sheridan proved that, surely? She had feelings, deep feelings. Or were they shallow, as Paul said? He had been a houseman then on general medical at the hospital where she had trained, but was interested in psychiatry. His uncle had been a psychiatrist and he had inherited the man's textbooks. That didn't make him an expert, and she had told him so. Yet the feeling persisted that Paul could be right; all she was capable of was a shallow sexual attraction. If a man wanted more than a pretty smile or a kiss she would back away. Hadn't she done so already?

She got out of bed, switched on the light, and gazed in the mirror. Worry lent a deep brilliance to the green eyes and there were shadows under them, she noted with distaste. The light dusting of freckles on her pert little nose seemed, to her anxious gaze, to have multiplied, and she turned away, wondering if frigidity showed in one's face.

Eventually she returned to her lonely bed. Heavy-hearted, she drifted off to sleep, hearing Paul's laughter in her mind, but seeing Adam's face.

The ward round went very well next day. Dr Sheridan was in an excellent mood, treating Isobel to a rare smile. The smile even reached those usually cold eyes, and Isobel rather wished he was his normal self. If he was happy it was solely because of Miss Kenlow.

As he was leaving after the round, she asked about Mrs Chipchase. He had paid the woman a brief visit as usual, but hadn't mentioned the possible vacancy in a Home. Mrs Chipchase's eyes had asked the question her tongue would not, but the consultant seemed not to notice. Now Isobel felt she must ask it for her.

'Mrs Chipchase, sir,' she said breathlessly. He paused in the doorway, then stood aside to let David Hanington and the house doctor go. He stood waiting, and Isobel hurried on: 'Yesterday Mrs Chipchase said you might have something in mind for her, but you didn't mention it this morning and I just wondered . . .' Her soft voice trailed off as his lips tightened. Now she'd put him in a bad mood, something she often did without knowing how or why.

'I'm working on it, Staff Nurse,' he said shortly, 'There are obstacles in the way at present, but . . .'

Isobel waited as he seemed to struggle for the right words. He sighed then, and her eyes darkened with sympathy. The poor man was tired and she had no right to detain him.

'David tells me you've asked him to give a lecture on multiple sclerosis to your ward nurses,' he went on, to her surprise, and she nodded.

'Yes, sir. I hope you don't mind? He said he would have to mention it to you. I thought it would be helpful,' she hurried on, prepared if necessary to defend her request.

'Your eyes sparkled then, Nurse.' He smiled, his grey eyes softening from their usual flinty hardness, and Isobel's heart started pounding.

'I was prepared to do battle with you, sir! I thought you objected to my asking Dr Hanington.'

'I object to your not asking *me*. It's the registrar's prerogative to give lectures in the school of nursing—paid lectures. I feel that it's mine to provide the occasional unpaid ones,' he explained, his eyes on her flushed face.

They fixed a date for the following week, and Isobel carefully noted it down in the ward diary, in her neat round hand. 'I may have some news about that vacancy when I see you next week,' he remarked as she finished writing.

He leaned forward and she raised her face to his, hoping he wouldn't hear the quickened beat of her heart. For a long moment they surveyed each other, Isobel feasting her eyes greedily upon that handsome, strong-featured face. She coloured under his continued scrutiny and he chuckled, a husky, sensual sound.

'It all depends on Miss Kenlow. The vacancy, I mean,' he said quietly.

The spell was broken, and Isobel's lips quivered as he left. Everything, it seemed, depended upon Miss Kenlow.

CHAPTER TWO

ISOBEL was free all day Saturday and was determined to make the most of it. Highcastle was a smallish town, but it boasted a theatre, and she had a ticket for the Saturday matinee, given her by a patient's daughter.

The play was adequate, no more than that, and did nothing to ease her heartache. She found her attention centred on Dr Sheridan rather than on the play. His moods seemed to hinge upon Miss Kenlow's. Since her appearance on Wednesday, he had been more alive, pleasant even. And Miss Kenlow held the key to this mysterious possible vacancy. Did she, Isobel wondered, own a Home of some sort? She might be a Matron, for all Isobel knew, though she doubted it.

'Isobel! What are you going in the town, pet?' It was David Hanington, looking faintly out of place.

'Don't tell me you've been playgoing!' Isobel laughed, and he nodded glumly, his tousled fair hair receiving another rake-through from his long, bony fingers.

'Aye, and on my own, too. Why didn't you say you were coming?'

'Why didn't you?' she countered, and he grinned sheepishly.

'We're not threatregoers around these parts. Lynne had tickets and she's on duty, so she sent me on my own,' he added, and Isobel looked her surprise. 'I wouldn't have come. I could have spent a cosy day in the park or lounging on a street corner somewhere and pretended I'd seen the play, but she'll want to know about it. She's keen on theatricals,' he explained. 'Why don't you join me for a bite?'

'I'd love to, but isn't Lynne expecting you?'

He shook his head. 'She's on late shift. She'll get something in the canteen.'

Pleased at the unexpected and welcome company, Isobel followed David through the Saturday crowds and allowed him to shepherd her to a small, discreetly-lit restaurant that had recently opened. Knowing that money wasn't that plentiful, she chose a salad followed by strawberry mousse, while David ploughed through an enormous plateful of braised chops.

They were sipping coffee when Isobel felt, rather than saw, Adam Sheridan. It was almost physical, the intensity of his gaze, and she half turned, that prickle of awareness already telling her he was nearby.

He sat alone at the bar, out of David's sight. Out of hers, too, unless she made the effort. He glanced up as he paid for his drink. Their eyes met, held, then he glanced away without apparently registering that it was her.

Isobel felt deflated. He must know it was her, he must! Out of uniform she looked different, of course. She had decided to dress up for the theatre even though it was afternoon, and her pale pearl-grey suit was new. With it she wore a lemon silk blouse, a colour which turned the red-brown hair to fire. Even so, he must have recognised her. She had felt his eyes upon her even before she had turned. Certainly he would recognise his tall registrar, whose attention was on his coffee.

She gazed down at her coffee cup, seeming to see the consultant's face floating there. Feeling foolish, she drained the coffee without tasting it.

David leaned back, giving his stomach a satisfied pat. 'That was what I call a meal! Lynne doesn't like eating out. This is the only place she'll come.'

Isobel smiled, glad the hard-working registrar had enjoyed the meal. Naturally she offered to pay for her own meal, but when the offer was refused she didn't press the point. She could repay David by inviting him and his wife for a home-cooked meal at the flat, something she often did. Even if she was incapable and less than a woman in other directions, she could cook!

'Who are you fighting?' There was laughter in David's eyes. Then he, too, saw Dr Sheridan. 'Don't look now, but that's our miserly old chief over there!' He jerked his head in the direction of the bar.

'I know. He did glance our way, but I don't think he recognised us. Unless he didn't want to,' she added, but David would hear no evil of his chief.

'He's not one to stand on his pedestal and ignore the rest of us. If he'd seen us he would have waved,' he insisted.

Isobel couldn't imagine the autocratic Dr Sheridan waving to someone across a crowded restaurant, but she let it pass.

David rose and lumbered over to the consultant. At that moment a tall, slender brunette paused by the door, then spoke to the head waiter. All at once Isobel knew who she was, even before the woman made her way purposefully to the bar and Adam Sheridan. This was the mysterious Miss Kenlow.

David swung round, managing to stand on the woman's toe as he did so, and Isobel winced in sympathy as Miss Kenlow shrieked in pain.

All eyes turned towards the scene, and Isobel felt embarrassed for David as he apologised profusely. Her eyes met Adam's and their gaze held for a long moment. It was as if they were alone. The crowded restaurant was empty, the tall, bumbling registrar and the elegant fiancée had vanished, only those two remained in all the world.

Dr Sheridan seemed to recall himself, and gently assisted the brunette to a chair, Isobel apparently forgotten. With a sad smile she picked up her coffee spoon, twirling it around and around, eyes downcast. She didn't want to see the tender solicitude Adam showed for his fiancée. She didn't need to. There was no doubt at all that he would be whispering gentle, soothing words into Miss Kenlow's ear, calming her down, enquiring after her injury. She was the sort of woman who would expect that kind of attention as a matter of right. Although tall, several inches taller than Isobel, she was slender, delicately built, looking as if the merest puff of wind would bowl her over.

The kind of woman who turned strong men to jelly, Isobel thought, without rancour. Although tiny and slim herself she was capable, as nurses must be. It was true that boy-friends in the past had certainly been eager to offer her a shoulder to cry on, including Paul Ashe, but she could not see the frosty-eyed consultant seeing her as delicate and in need of protection! She was a nurse, handmaiden to the doctor, useful in her place, but definitely not a woman. She felt there were three sexes to Adam Sheridan—male, female, and nurse!

A red-faced David Hanington sat down heavily in his chair and she gave him a sympathetic smile.

'It would have to be the chief's girl-friend!' he said ruefully, turning to gaze at the pair. Isobel did likewise. The couple were sitting at a secluded table now, with the waiter hovering. Isobel's eyes darkened with a sadness she could not have explained. Fortunately David did not notice, and seemed in a hurry to leave.

Wistfully she gazed at the other two, aware that they could not see her. Perhaps they were having an early dinner before the evening performance of the play. Theatregoing was a pleasure to be shared if possible. Paul hadn't cared for it, although he had endured the occasional concert for her sake.

When she had suggested, hopefully, that they might visit the Barbican for a Shakespeare performance, he had refused. As it was nearly her twenty-second birthday and he had promised her an evening out she had been cross with him and they had exchanged angry words. But one look at his desperately weary face and she had begged his forgiveness for her selfishness. He was only a house doctor then, though he had since become a registrar, and house doctors worked long hours. It was understandable that he didn't want to spend his free evening watching a play he hated. She could not expect it of him, even for the girl he professed to love—though in a moment of insight she had reflected that if there was anything for him after the show, sex in payment for her evening out, he would have willingly gone to commune with the Bard!

She and David parted company, he to return home, she to make her way back to her lonely flat. After that unexpected moment of rapport, that exchanged glance across a crowded room, the flat would seem lonelier than ever.

Monday brought a new admission, a patient with myocardial infarction transferred from ITU. Mrs Dean was in her sixties, a tall, plump lady with hair that was only slightly grey. She had gained the reputation of being complaining and difficult, and Isobel was wary as she and the first-year student helped her into bed.

'At least this is a step in the right direction,' Student Nurse Ruddock assured her cheerfully, and Isobel winced, the more so when Mrs Dean retorted: 'I suppose a step in the wrong direction would be the mortuary!'

The student looked nonplussed, wondering if it was meant as a joke, but Isobel shook her head warningly. Gently she explained to Mrs Dean about visiting times and told her a little of the ward routine—something that was too often overlooked. Patients became anxious unless they knew the times of meals or times when they could expect a familiar face coming from home. Isobel also explained that she wasn't the Ward Sister but that

Sister Sowerby would be back on duty the following Sunday.

'Sister will expect a definite improvement by then, Mrs Dean,' she went on firmly, 'though you've made tremendous strides already. Your husband must be pleased.'

The patient's face lit up. 'Have I really made tremendous strides? I thought . . .' Her voice trailed away wearily, and Isobel squeezed her hand. The rest of the conversation could keep until later.

Adam Sheridan was aware of Mrs Dean's move and would be along as soon as he was able, she knew, her heart quickening its beat at the prospect of seeing him again. It was all so silly! By Sunday morning she had convinced herself that she had imagined that enchanted moment in the restaurant, that moment when she and Adam were the only people in the world. It was pure fancy on her part that they had shared something wonderful, an interlude in which the beautiful Miss Kenlow had no place.

Nevertheless, fancy or not, she awaited his arrival with eager anticipation. The man didn't like her, and he certainly didn't see her other than as a nurse. Still . . .

Isobel was instructing Nurse Ruddock on myocardial infarctions when Dr Sheridan appeared. Teaching was something she enjoyed, and she sometimes thought about becoming a clinical instructor if she didn't apply for a Sister's post. Yet she felt she would lose contact with the patients. Although clinical instructors worked on the wards, they were set apart and could not have the same sense of belonging as Sister or staff nurse, the same sense of pleased relief when a patient was discharged fit or nearly so.

All in all she preferred the bustle of her own ward but still liked to teach whenever she could. A new patient always provided a good opportunity.

'It isn't always necessary for a patient with myocardial infarction to be admitted to Intensive Care,' she explained. 'Sometimes they come straight to the ward, but we're not really equipped to deal with the serious cases. Mrs Dean was very poorly and didn't seem likely to survive long, so she went to ITU for a few days. She's on the mend now, but she must be kept quiet and not allowed to exert herself.'

'When will she be allowed up, Staff?' Nurse Ruddock wanted to know. 'She seems rather a discontented lady,' she added reflectively.

'She'll probably be happier once she's up and about,' Isobel replied, though privately doubting that it would alter the woman's personality. Mrs Dean was a perfectionist, insisting that everything was done the correct way—*her* way, naturally. Myocardial infarction was more common among men, but Mrs Dean held what might be termed a man's job. She had a responsible managerial post which presumably included going for long and heavy company meals, and it was this type who was the standard candidate for an infarction, or coronary thrombosis, as it used to be termed.

'It shouldn't be long before she's up and sitting by her bed, but it will be only for short periods at first. It depends on what Dr Sheridan thinks of her,'

Isobel carried on, then her eyes widened in surprise as the plump and pretty Nurse Ruddock rose hastily, smiling shyly at someone behind Isobel.

She ought to have realised it was Adam Sheridan. For once her antennae had let her down. She had been so carried away by her teaching that her senses hadn't quivered in their usual manner when he appeared!

She too, rose, prepared to dismiss the young student so he could consult the patient's notes in peace and quiet.

He put up a restraining hand as Nurse Ruddock reluctantly moved away. 'Carry on with the good work, Staff Nurse.' His tone was amiable for once, and perversely Isobel was cross.

'As you wish, sir,' she said stiffly, causing those grey eyes to narrow shrewdly. Even Nurse Ruddock looked surprised at the coldness of Isobel's tone.

Without a word she handed the consultant Mrs Dean's case notes, then continued her lecture on the woman's myocardial infarction. 'It may be three months or so before Mrs Dean can resume her job.' Isobel's voice was quiet, controlled now. Her annoyance at Adam had quickly evaporated. If Miss Kenlow could turn the usually austere Dr Sheridan into a meek lamb, who was she to complain? 'She may need a less strenuous job, though. Or perhaps she could resume the one she has but on a part-time basis.'

'She won't be a permanent invalid, then?' Nurse Ruddock found her voice at last. Though clearly overawed by the consultant's presence, she was keen to know more, and was busily scribbling in the small notebook she carried in her uniform pocket.

'I hope not. Certainly once the infarct has healed she should become moderately active again. Some exercise is better than none at all. She must be encouraged to lead as normal a life as possible. She ought to give up smoking, though,' she added, almost to herself.

'She was asking the auxiliary for one. I heard her,' Nurse Ruddock volunteered, and Adam glanced up sharply.

'There's no smoking on the ward! Surely the stupid woman realises that?' Those dark brows drew together in a heavy frown. Adam Sheridan was back to normal.

'I . . . oh yes, sir. Of course she does, sir,' the student spluttered, going red.

Such patients were not allowed to smoke during their stay in hospital and seldom felt like a cigarette, anyway. Upon discharge they were advised against the habit, but the staff could do no more than warn. The same stricture applied to heavy meals and excessive alcohol, plus stress. All these factors had contributed to Mrs Dean's illness.

'What *is* a myocardial infarction, Nurse? Do you know?' Adam asked suddenly, and the student hesitated for a moment while Isobel died a thousand deaths, wondering if she had explained that ill-important fact.

Then Nurse Ruddock nodded emphatically. 'Oh, yes, I know, sir. We covered heart diseases in school and Staff Nurse always explains whatever we don't understand.' She paused, and Isobel encouraged her to continue. 'It's the damage and death of heart muscle. The myocardium is the muscle tissue of the heart, sir.'

She seemed unsure of her ground, and Isobel put in: 'Tell Doctor what it is that damages the myocardium. That's very important.'

'It's caused by a blood vessel being blocked. By . . . by plaques,' the student stumbled on. She was staring straight ahead, apparently calling to her mind the relevant pages of her textbook. She must have been successful, for she finished hurriedly: 'The coronary arteries are narrowed by deposits of fatty material, and this may cause the blood to clot in the narrowed artery or the artery might become clogged up by the deposits. The heart muscle is cut off from its blood supply and that part of it dies.' The student let out a hearty sigh once she had hurried through the rest of her answer, and Dr Sheridan smiled at her.

Isobel noticed that the cleft in his chin deepened when he smiled, and wondered wistfully if he would ever smile like that at her. 'You seem to have the right idea, Nurse,' he acknowledged, and admiration shone out of the girl's eyes.

Isobel sent her off to see Mrs Dean, then stood quietly as Adam Sheridan perused the woman's notes.

'Heavy smoker and hearty eater, by the sound of it,' he commented dryly.

'She's a big businesswoman, sir. I suppose she feels she has to keep up with the men—become one of the boys!'

He glanced up and their eyes met. She wondered

what was going on in his mind. His hooded gaze gave nothing away, and she hoped her own eyes were equally expressionless.

'Do you feel you have to keep up with the men, Staff Nurse?'

Isobel, thrown, could only stare, but he seemed not to expect an answer. He went on reflectively: 'It's particularly hard for a woman in a man's world. Women are sensitive creatures and nature didn't intend them to be cold and calculating, ruthless.'

'No, sir,' she murmured, wondering if he was thinking of Miss Kenlow.

'I was thinking of an old friend of mine. She's got MS and it's cut off her career in its prime. She had her own business at one time. She's a similar personality, I should think, to this Mrs Dean. That's why I thought of her.'

'It's the active, full of life people it attacks,' Isobel mused. She thought to mention her friend who had multiple sclerosis, but decided he would be too busy to listen. Avril, her best friend at training school, had some of the symptoms, but was at present in a long period of remission. It had ruined the girl's nursing career, and it was because of her that Isobel herself had become interested in the disease, reading up on it and trying, for her friend's sake, to seek out a cure. Research might provide an answer to it in the near future and there were some hopeful signs, but at present there was no cure.

'There's no cure at the moment.' Adam might have been reading her mind, and Isobel blushed.

He watched with apparent interest as the warm

tide of colour suffused her neck and cheeks, and she momentarily closed her eyes in embarrassment. The freckles were, she felt, standing out on stalks. He had no right to stare at her like that!

'You're very pretty when you blush, Nurse Ford,' he commented, causing her more anguish. 'Extraordinarily so', he added softly.

Her eyes snapped open and she glared at him. 'I'm glad you think so!' she said hotly, hating herself for losing her control and hating him for provoking her, even if it *was* accidental.

He moved nearer and she held her breath. Those chilly grey eyes were warm now. In their depths lurked passion, she was sure of it. It was ridiculous. The man was engaged! He hadn't the right to look at another woman like that.

With a supreme effort of will she glanced away and began quietly tidying the desk. He still held Mrs Dean's notes and she asked him, in a soft, controlled voice, whether he was ready to see the woman.

'What made you come up to these wild northern climes?' he asked, ignoring her question.

Isobel hesitated, wondering what he would say if he knew about Paul Ashe and about Paul's diagnosis of her. 'I wanted a change, sir. It's . . . it's a long way from London and it's a complete change of scenery, too. The countryside here is beautiful,' she went on.

'I doubt that you came all this way just to see the countryside', he said brusquely. 'Come on, I haven't all day. I'll see Mrs Dean now.'

Face flaming, Isobel followed him from the office. He couldn't know there was a man involved in her flight from the south, yet he'd guessed. It displeased him for some reason, and Isobel wondered why.

CHAPTER THREE

MRS DEAN continued to make slow progress and Adam appeared satisfied with her. Another attack could, naturally, occur at any time, and Isobel warned her nurses to be on the lookout for the telltale signs, particularly the development of cardiac dysrhythmia. Chest pain at rest, too, was an important symptom.

It was now Saturday and Sister Sowerby was due back the next day. Isobel sat at the desk, her mind half on the imminent return of her senior, half on her patients. The ward was quiet, uncannily so, and it worried her. The calm before the storm, she remembered thinking, then there was a brisk tap at the door and a tall brunette appeared, wafting in on a cloud of heady perfume.

Isobel's eyes widened as she recognised Miss Kenlow—Adam Sheridan's Miss Kenlow.

The visitor smiled vaguely in Isobel's direction. 'I'm trying to find Dr Sheridan, Nurse.' Her voice was light and melodious—rather pleasant, Isobel conceded. And she was beautiful, very beautiful.

She explained that Dr Sheridan wasn't usually on the ward at weekends. 'His secretary works Saturday mornings, though. I could ring her for you. Is it personal?' she added, knowing very well.

Miss Kenlow bestowed a chilly smile on her, then her china blue eyes narrowed thoughtfully as they read Isobel's name-badge. 'So *you* are the little redheaded staff nurse Adam talks about! I imagined someone *older*.' Before Isobel could recover her speech, she went on: 'I'm Miss Sonia Kenlow. Perhaps you've heard of me?'

'Well, yes,' Isobel agreed. 'You're a friend of Dr Sheridan's.'

'More than a friend, my dear!' Miss Kenlow purred. 'His fiancée!'

Isobel glanced at the woman's ring finger and was pleased to find it bare of rings. 'I'm afraid I still can't help you. I don't know Doctor's movements at weekends,' she added, wondering why his fiancée should imagine he was in the hospital.

Miss Kenlow shrugged. 'I suppose he's with Mrs Bland,' she muttered peevishly.

'Mrs Bland?'

'She has multiple sclerosis. She's an old friend of Adam's,' Miss Kenlow explained. 'It's a damn nuisance! Never mind, I'll try there.' She hurried away, annoyance in the way she held herself, and Isobel sat back in relief. She wouldn't want to get on the wrong side of *her*!

So he didn't tell his fiancée where he spent his weekends. It seemed odd. Surely he would want to spend them with his intended? Mrs Bland, presumably, was the MS patient Adam had mentioned previously, the one with a dominating personality like Mrs Dean.

Isobel felt lonelier than ever after Miss Kenlow had departed. Sonia Kenlow had Adam Sheridan. She had no one. Fleeing from one's problems and heartbreak wasn't such a good idea. She was still the same person, still the apparently frigid Nurse Ford Paul had taunted. Yet despite his unkindnesses, absence *did* make the heart grow fonder. She began to wonder what Paul was doing right now, whether he had found another love, a warmer one. There would be no shortage of candidates for his love.

For a few seconds she was tempted to get in touch with him, ask him how he was getting on in his new registrar's post. But the urge passed. After his unkind, harsh words to her she never wanted to see the man again. She didn't *care* how he was getting on!

That afternoon Mrs Dean had a visitor, her sister, who assured Isobel that Mrs Dean was only too eager to co-operate with the nurses if it hastened her recovery, but Isobel doubted that. So far, the patient had been far from co-operative. She could not understand why she wasn't allowed out of bed, insisting that she felt fit again. When Adam was told of her restlessness and keenness to be up and about he had reluctantly allowed the woman to sit out of bed for ten minutes. Not that that stopped Mrs Dean complaining! She complained about the small, nourishing meals, all the fluids she was encouraged to drink, about the lack of privacy, and especially about not being able to smoke.

Once she was out of danger Isobel intended that she should be given the side room, their most private one, if Sister agreed. She wondered why a businesswoman like Mrs Dean hadn't gone into a private clinic, but perhaps a move to a clinic was on the cards for later. At the moment she was too ill to undertake such a journey, and there wasn't a private clinic nearby.

Isobel resolved to have a word with her once

visiting time was over, but the patients weren't the only ones to receive visitors. She had one herself.

For her it was a long day. She had been on duty part of the morning, then had a long lunch break before continuing for the rest of the afternoon and evening.

SEN Mackenzie rang the bell signalling the end of visiting time, but, as always, one or two people lingered, reluctant to end their visit. Mrs Dean's sister wasn't one of these, however, and she left promptly. As yet Mrs Dean wasn't allowed full visiting rights. She could have only one visitor at a time, and then only the closest of relatives. The time allowed was only half an hour, less if the patient seemed to be fatigued. Her husband would probably visit tomorrow afternoon, Isobel mused, making for the door. She must see if the woman needed anything.

Busy with her thoughts, she didn't notice the tall man about to enter the office, and they collided. The breath was knocked out of her and her cap slid gracefully over her right ear. She began to apologise, supposing him to be a late visitor, then she was shaken gently, and she focused at last. 'Paul!' she gasped.

Dr Paul Ashe released her, then adjusted her cap. He smiled down at her. He was just as handsome, as charming as she remembered. It was as if the last twelve months had never been. At that moment she was prepared to forgive him all the heartache he had caused her.

He wasn't quite as tall as Adam Sheridan, she noted, wondering why the darkly handsome consultant should spring to mind. Paul's eyes were a deep, vivid blue as against the sombre grey, almost black, of the older man. He was better looking, though, she conceded, her eyes softening against her will. And much more charming!

She knew it was foolish to allow the love light to leap into her eyes, but she was human. She couldn't help responding to Paul's charm, his warmth, his obvious pleasure in seeing her again.

'I've missed you, Isobel,' he said simply, and she could not doubt his sincerity. It was something for him to admit missing anyone; he was one of the most self-sufficient people she knew. Dr Ashe didn't need anyone, and it was a thrill to know that he had actually missed little Nurse Ford!

Hesitantly, she invited him to sit in the office while she made a round of the patients. The last visitor was just leaving as she made her way down the ward. Mrs Dean's bed was first, the nearest to the office, but she appeared to be sleeping. She looked drawn and weary, and Isobel paused to check on her. Automatically her fingers reached for Mrs Dean's wrist—although her pulse was checked four-hourly, another check would do no harm. The patient's eyes opened and she gazed at Isobel, seemingly without recognition.

'I'm Staff Nurse Ford, Mrs Dean,' Isobel reminded her. 'Is everything all right? Did your visitor tire you?'

'Yes, she did. She's tired me ever since I've known her.' The patient's tone was peevish.

'If you don't want visitors for a few days I can keep them away,' Isobel offered gently. 'Your husband will be coming tomorrow, I expect.'

'I'll see how I feel then. I'm so terribly tired.' Her

eyes closed again and Isobel continued on her tour.
If she hurried straight back to the office Mrs Dean
might become agitated and worried, but once she'd
seen all the other patients she intended phoning
the duty doctor. It would do no harm. Suddenly
she longed for the reassuring figure of Dr Adam
Sheridan, but alas, she could not conjure him up.

Mrs Chipchase had been visited by someone
from the Multiple Sclerosis Society and she too was
lying with her eyes closed, so Isobel didn't disturb
her.

She had almost forgotten Paul, and her eyes lit
up when she realised he was still there. Then she
smiled sadly. He was busily engaged charming
Aimee Ruddock. He hadn't changed, she
reflected. Hastily the student left the office, her
face flushed, and Isobel eyed him sternly. 'I hope
you haven't been flirting with my staff, Dr Ashe.
You'll turn Nurse Ruddock's head.'

His face creased into a smile. 'You know me,
darling. Love 'em and leave 'em!' he joked, and she
felt there was some truth in that. 'Anyway—*veni,
vidi, vici!*'

'Quite.' Her tone was dry, and Paul chuckled.

'No, not the tubby little student. You!'

Isobel raised a brow. 'You came all this way to
conquer me, did you? I find *that* hard to believe.'

He avoided her gaze. 'Actually, no. I'm in
Newcastle at a conference. It's rather boring, but it
makes a change from hospital life.'

'And you thought you would pop in to see me as
you were passing?' she suggested, but he indignantly denied that.

'No! I *wanted* to see you again, Isobel. Honestly.'

His expression was pained, but she had no more time to spare for him.

'I've work to do now, Paul. I've a rather poorly patient.' Ignoring his sigh, she arranged for the duty doctor to be bleeped. Then Nurse Mackenzie appeared and was introduced to Paul. She appeared unmoved by his charm and he looked crestfallen as he left. He was going to pick her up after duty, but Isobel wasn't sure she wanted to go anywhere. It had been a long day, an extra shift to work, and she wanted a hot bath and an early night with a novel, preferably with a hero who resembled Adam Sheridan! She frowned, wondering why her ideal hero was the chilly, distant and often un-pleasant Adam Sheridan when the man she supposedly loved was completely different.

To pass away the time until the doctor answered his bleep she got out Mrs Dean's notes, then a white-faced Nurse Ruddock came rushing in. 'Please, Staff—it's Mrs Dean!' She hurried out again before Isobel could speak. Icy fingers trailed up and down her spine as she followed the student. The duty doctor might be too late.

Her worst fears were realised as she glanced at the patient. Nurse Mackenzie was already on her way to the office to put out the emergency call which would bring the resus team post-haste. Mrs Dean had stopped breathing. Her face was grey and sweaty, her eyes vacant.

'She said her chest was hurting, Staff.' Nurse Ruddock's voice seemed to come from far away as Isobel began the vital resuscitation measures. If resuscitation wasn't started within three minutes irreversible brain damage would occur. Even seconds were vital. Yet she couldn't ask the first-year student to help other than to draw the curtains. She hissed at her to fetch all available help, then began the so-called 'kiss of life'.

Luckily the woman had her own teeth. If she'd worn dentures valuable time would have been lost while these were removed. Isobel extended the woman's neck to allow a clear airway, then pinched the patient's nose to keep it closed and blew into her mouth. It was hard work, the more so because she had to begin the cardiac massage as well until Nurse Mackenzie dashed back. Then she was moved aside as Joy Mackenzie took over the exhaled air resuscitation and Sister from Male Medical next door carried on with the cardiac massage.

Isobel took in long gulps of air. Her head was swimming and she had the awful sensation that came just before a faint. She didn't, but it was a near thing.

The resus team arrived and the nurses stood aside. Two porters appeared, almost hurling the resus trolley into the ward, and Isobel sent up a prayer of thankfulness as expert preparations began.

Luckily there was already a fracture board on Mrs Dean's bed. If a board hadn't been procured immediately the patient would have had to be resuscitated on the floor, as a hard surface was vitally important. Pillows and bedclothes were hurled aside as Isobel and a porter removed the head of the bed to allow easier access.

The team included an anaesthetist, and Isobel watched as he began intubation, the insertion of a tube into Mrs Dean's larynx which would allow inflation of her lungs by oxygen. She helped set up the drip which would run Sodium Bicarbonate into the patient's veins to counter the acidosis which occurred during a cardiac arrest.

She spared a hurried glance at her staff. SEN Mackenzie appeared in complete control and was co-ordinating the other nurses while Isobel herself assisted the team. Nurse Ruddock was comforting the other patients, though Isobel doubted that a badly frightened first-year could offer much comfort. The third-year, Ann Peters, had been loaned out to Male Medical, but she was back now, observing the drama, learning what to do for the future.

Once more Isobel wished for Adam Sheridan's commanding presence, and suddenly he was there. He and David Hanington began the defibrillating.

An electrocardiograph had been taken and it showed that Mrs Dean's heart was now beating, but it was a weak, unco-ordinated beat, called fibrillation. If there hadn't been a beat, intra-cardiac adrenalin would have been given, the drug being injected straight into the heart. This might have restored a normal beat or induced the unco-ordinated beat that now presented the problem.

The treatment for a fibrillating heart was an electric shock, more than one if absolutely necessary. This was called defibrillation, and ought to set the heart beating properly again. The heart could not do its vital work of pumping the blood around the body otherwise.

Isobel watched Adam and David put on their rubber gloves for protection. The paddle electrodes were smeared with jelly, then applied to Mrs

Dean's skin. This was how the shock would be administered. Adam Sheridan glanced quickly around. 'Stand clear,' he ordered, and Isobel pulled Nurse Peters farther back. Everyone had to keep well clear of the bed and patient as the electric current was passed, otherwise they would receive an unpleasant electric shock.

The shock, of low voltage, worked first time and the woman's heart resumed its normal rhythm. If the heart hadn't responded to the first dose, further shocks would have been given in rapid succession and repeated at a higher voltage if absolutely necessary.

'ITU,' Adam ordered, but Nurse Mackenzie was already on her way, taking Nurse Peters with her. She would ring ITU and warn them that they were about to have Mrs Dean back. Mrs Dean was wheeled out on the bed by the resus team to spare her system the ordeal of being transferred to a trolley, then back into a bed once she arrived at ITU. It was a matter of urgency that she got to ITU as soon as possible.

Isobel collected her notes and personal items and sent Nurse Mackenzie off with them. Wearily, she glanced around at the patients. Those who could were sitting up, peering at the space where Mrs Dean's bed had stood only seconds before.

She laughed shakily. 'That was an experience I don't want to repeat, so the rest of you ladies had better recover quickly!'

There were relieved smiles and laughter from the patients, and the hum of conversation started again, the usual sound on a medical ward, and Isobel relaxed, but only for a moment. There was still Mr Dean to be told. She hoped the news wouldn't give him a heart attack!

Although she had been strong and supportive throughout the crisis, reaction set in once all the extra duties were carried out. She felt faint again and rather sick. Yet she must see to her young nurses. That was a joke! Nurse Peters was only a few months younger than her, but training and experience created a gap between them.

She found Nurse Ruddock in the sluice, having a good cry as she prepared the bedpan trolley. Isobel let her cry, knowing how it relieved pent-up emotions. She could have done with one herself.

When the flood of tears passed, she helped the girl wheel out the heavy trolley, reminding her to put on her rubber apron to protect her uniform.

Nurse Peters had seen only one cardiac arrest before and was anxious to fill in the gaps in her knowledge. She was older than the other students and had, she confided, taken up nursing when she was made redundant from her previous job! Isobel liked her. The girl had more than proved her worth and she took her duties very seriously. Her face was gravely attentive as a weary Isobel tried to answer her questions.

'That blow on the sternum, Staff Nurse—it might have been enough to start the heart beating again?'

'Yes. Sometimes the blow sets it off, but as you saw, it didn't this time.'

'And the acidosis, Staff? Is it right that . . .'

'For God's sake, let Staff Nurse rest!' Neither girl had been aware of the door opening wider. Now they turned with one accord, and Isobel's heart skipped a beat. She didn't know what it was she felt for Adam Sheridan, but whatever the emotion, it was strong! She loved Paul Ashe, at least she did once. Hadn't she mourned him for a whole year? She did not, of course, love the icy Adam Sheridan, but nevertheless there was something almost tangible in the air as she smiled at him.

'It's all right. Really, sir. Nurse Peters is anxious to learn and . . .'

'And I'm anxious that you should finish tidying up, hand over the ward and go off duty,' he rejoined, holding open the door for Nurse Peters.

Once the student had left, he swiftly crossed over to Isobel, who stood, her legs unable to propel her anywhere.

'Sit down before you fall down.' His voice was harsh, uncompromising, and she obeyed. Once she sat down she was afraid she wouldn't have the strength to rise. She was desperately tired, mentally as well as physically. Dr Sheridan had no right to shout at her, no right at all. She ought to tell him so, but her mouth felt dry and her tongue and lips could not form the words.

Instead, she managed a heartfelt sigh. Her eyelids closed of their own accord and she allowed herself a few seconds to recover. 'I feel better now,' she told him, struggling to open her eyes again. The right eye remained obstinately closed and the left one closed again in sympathy. From a long way off she heard a husky chuckle. Something touched her eyelids briefly, tenderly, like the kiss of swansdown, or the merest breeze, and suddenly she was wide awake.

Adam Sheridan was standing over her, his gaze concerned. Face flushed, she rose. What she had felt on her lids was a kiss, she was almost sure. Yet it couldn't be. The distinguished, chilly Adam Sheridan wouldn't be guilty of such an act! It was most unprofessional and she was, after all, a mere lazy good-for-nothing southerner.

Her eyes flashed green fire at him, and he chuckled, making her angrier than ever. He had no business laughing at her!

'I suppose if I was one of your robust Geordies I wouldn't feel weary now!' she flared, forgetting her training for once. She wanted to lash out at him— why, she could not have said.

He stepped back as though struck. Amazement was written all over his face. Probably no mere staff nurse had ever dared speak to him like that before.

'I'm sorry,' she muttered.

'That can be arranged!' he snapped. 'You may be very sorry indeed at a later date. However, I haven't time to argue with silly young girls— southerners *or* Geordies,' he emphasised, and Isobel felt ashamed. He didn't deserve the remark she'd flung at him. He would have disliked her just as much if she had been a Tynesider like himself, she realised. The man disliked her and there was no more to be said—hadn't he made it plain enough this past twelve months? A whole year of working in close contact with him and never a kind word, a shared smile, a friendly gesture.

Tears pricked her eyelids, a weak gesture she knew he would not appreciate. Hastily she blinked them away, avoiding his searching gaze.

'Isobel?' The name was a question and a caress in one, and she looked up, the lovely green eyes bright with those weak, womanly tears.

Those cold eyes gave nothing away. She'd read about an unfathomable gaze; now she knew what it meant. Whatever emotion he was capable of, nothing of it showed. The man was a marble statue. He didn't *have* feelings.

'Oh, Bella, what shall we do with you?' he sighed, and she eyed him in astonishment. 'Send you home is the only course possible, I think.'

'My name is Isobel, sir!' she blurted out.

'Bella is a Geordie name. It's earthier than Isobel,' he chuckled. His eyes warmed, briefly, then the flinty hardness returned to them, the shutter came down. 'Isobel sounds rather a prim and proper sort of name,' he added. 'Rather cold.'

He could not have known how those words struck home like an arrow piercing her heart. Rather cold—like her. Frigid, as Paul Ashe had said. A cold name for a cold lady.

She summoned a smile, the tightness in her chest almost a physical pain. If he had tried, he could not have hurt her more, but he wasn't to blame. 'I think Isobel is a more suitable name for me, sir,' she said.

'Yes, you could be right,' he said reflectively, and she wished he had been interested enough to argue the point.

'I . . . I'd better finish the report, then I must tidy the desk.' Resolutely she got up, keen to show him she was fully recovered. It wasn't, after all, the first time she'd had to resuscitate a patient. She hardly dared ask how Mrs Dean was, afraid the news would be bad.

'She's holding on. I think she'll do,' the consultant reassured her. 'You spoke to the husband?'

'Mm, but he wasn't concerned. I don't think

they're all that close,' Isobel offered, and the dark brows frowned at her. 'I didn't mean he didn't care. He seemed to think she would be all right here. He said he knew we would look after her.'

'If *he* had looked after her, persuaded her to slow down, she might not have needed our help.' His tone was irritable. 'He's a similar type, though. Money-making is all. Happens too often in marriage.'

Startled, Isobel said: 'What does? Setting up money as a god?'

'No! The partners pulling in opposite directions. It makes a mockery of marriage. A wife should encourage her husband in his career, be a help-meet, not try to emulate him, become the female equivalent of a big businessman. It ruins marriages!'

His vehemence shocked her. As a nurse, she believed she could have a satisfying career and be a successful wife as well, until the children came along. It seemed to be a personal matter with him, though, and she wondered about Sonia Kenlow. Did the elegant lady have a career? If she did, was it more important to her than her impending marriage? Maybe it was a bone of contention between them. It could partly account for Adam's mood swings, the veiled hostility that emanated from him more often than not.

Sonia Kenlow wasn't making him happy. It didn't seem fair. He *deserved* a little happiness.

She finished her paperwork while he leafed through a patient's notes. They were Mrs Chipchase's notes and she wondered if there was any news, but she wouldn't ask him. When he was

in a mood he often ignored her questions. Sometimes she wondered why she put up with the man.
She could get a transfer to another ward, to another
hospital, even. There were one or two cottage
hospitals in the countryside. It would make a
pleasant change. Why should she put up with a
chauvinist like Adam Sheridan? Give yourself one
good reason, she argued.

Then her gaze dropped to his dark head, bent
over the notes. Unlike Paul Ashe, his hair was too
long—rather untidy, really. Paul was never untidy,
believing it important for an ambitious young doctor to be always immaculate. The prize was a
consultancy in due course, and Paul always had his
eyes on that prize, she knew.

Adam was tired. He ought not to be in the
hospital at all; he was entitled to his weekends off.
Her eyes softened and it was a good thing he did not
look up, otherwise he might have taken her fond,
sympathetic glance to mean rather more than it
did. It was simply concern on her part, nothing
more than tender loving care from a nurse to a
particularly trying yet endearing patient!

CHAPTER FOUR

'HERE we are, home at last!'

Isobel stirred in the seat beside Adam Sheridan. She had been dozing during the short drive but now came properly awake, eager to see what sort of house he lived in.

She wasn't quite sure how she came to be there. She couldn't remember agreeing to his suggestion of supper at his cottage. Probably he had not bothered to ask, she reflected without bitterness. He had simply taken her acquiescence for granted. Typical of the man!

He held open the car door for her and she stumbled in her tiredness, almost falling against him. He drew back as if burned; he couldn't bear her to touch him! She wanted to assure him that it was an accident, but already he was turning away.

Sighing, Isobel followed. It was still light, but only just, and the old detached house loomed, silent and grey. On the breeze she caught the faint aroma of some evening flower. It was still, tranquil. She paused before going inside, gazing up at the tall Victorian windows. It was a three-storied building, but she supposed there might be a cellar as was common in those times. There were two small attic windows just under the eaves. Part brick, part mellowed local stone, it had character and was the type of home she would have liked.

Adam Sheridan was standing by the solid oak

front door, impatience in every stern line of him, and she followed.

'Welcome to my home,' he said simply, and Isobel smiled at him. The words sounded welcoming enough even if he was already regretting his generous invitation. No doubt he was as tired as she was.

His eyes lingered on her face for a long moment, and she held her breath, wondering why her heart was jumping about. The man meant nothing to her, nothing at all. Whatever emotion he aroused in her breast, it was quite different from love or even a sexual wanting.

A half smile flickered across his dark face, then was gone; indeed, she might have imagined it. 'I'll put the coffee on and see what I can rustle up for supper. Have a look around. Make yourself at home,' he offered, then disappeared.

Make yourself at home—how good that sounded! Her eyes darkened, the green deepening to a deep, dark emerald. With an effort she pulled herself together and began her necessarily brief tour of Adam's home. Weariness overcame her as she climbed the narrow stairs, but she kept on, determined to see what she could on this her only visit. Begin at the top and work your way down, she thought.

The main upper storey consisted of three bedrooms, two of them double, plus a big bathroom with an enclosed shower unit. Isobel felt like an interloper as she peered into each room in turn. She came upon Adam's bedroom last, the one next to the bathroom. She hesitated in the doorway, feeling she would violate his privacy by going further.

It was a big room overlooking the rear garden. Her eyes roamed the room in search of some sign of female occupancy, and she hated herself for her inquisitiveness. There seemed to be none, however. It was a typical masculine bedroom. On the dark oak dressing-table by the window stood a silver-backed brush set. Despite her intention not to enter the room, she did so, drawn by a force stronger than herself.

Beside the brushes there were several glass trinket dishes. One contained an assortment of cufflinks, another an ornate gold tiepin. Then she caught the merest whiff of aftershave, the one Adam was using today, and she spun round, hot colour flooding her cheeks.

But she was alone, and she sank on to the bed for a moment, her heart pitter-pattering. The bed was huge, kingsize. It was just an ordinary bed otherwise—no fancy frills or lacy bedspread for him. The cover was brown and white, in keeping with the rest of the furnishings, all good solid furniture, homely.

Strangely reluctant to leave his room, she made her way to the safety of the pretty green and beige bathroom. There she found his bottle of aftershave, and matching talc and soap. Sonia Kenlow must have bought the set for him, otherwise he wouldn't have bothered, she felt; soap and water and a good deodorant would have been all he used. He looked the outdoor type, not a dapper city dweller with assorted colognes and perfumes and probably skin moisturiser as well.

Another, narrower staircase, stretched upwards invitingly from the landing. It must lead to the attic rooms. Isobel paused, then began the climb. She wouldn't be coming again and she wanted some memories to dwell on.

The attic room she came to first was furnished as a study, she saw, once her groping hand had found the light switch. A long desk took up most of the floor space, with bookshelves ranging the walls. To one side stood a small filing cabinet and she saw a portable typewriter under the window on a little table.

Switching out the light again, she crossed over to the high window and gazed out. The attic window overlooked the garden, but dusk was falling now and she could make out only the barest outlines—a shed, greenhouse, some shrubs and a lawn disappearing into the oncoming night. She thought she caught the glimmer of a stream but could not be sure.

Reluctant to leave yet knowing she mustn't outstay her welcome, she turned slowly—then caught her breath. The tall, muscular figure of Adam Sheridan stood just inside the room.

Unnerved, Isobel floundered: 'Sorry! I didn't realise I was taking so long. It's all very nice, very interesting,' she hurried on, as he continued to stand in silence, his expression inscrutable. 'I love old houses. My . . . my friend . . . a friend in London—his parents have a Victorian—Oh!' Paul. She'd forgotten their date! It was Paul's parents who owned a huge, rambling old house in a quiet London square. The house to which Paul Ashe might one day take his bride.

Her eyes saddened. To profess to love the man and then to forget a date with him was dreadful. It couldn't be love after all.

'Don't you want that coffee, Bella?' Adam Sheridan's voice was soft, sensuous, even, and she blushed.

'Oh! Oh, yes—yes, please. I suddenly remembered something. I'm just coming.'

He shrugged, evidently thinking weariness was making her stupider than usual, then he climbed down the narrow, twisting stairs.

Going down was much harder than going up, and her head felt woozy. She was tired—hungry, too. Her brain needed more sustenance than it had received today, and she stumbled when she was nearly down. Strong arms helped her the rest of the way. Her heart thudded unaccountably, and she wondered at that. Adam held her no longer than was absolutely necessary, though, and the palpitations stopped.

Coffee was waiting in the sitting room, a room that stretched the whole length of the house, probably two knocked into one. Isobel gazed about with interest, keen to avoid being too close to him. It was sparsely furnished with just a three-piece suite plus an additional wing chair, a buffet unit and a couple of occasional tables. Over in a corner a big television set sat discreetly, a bowl of roses perching on top. She seized on that. 'Are the roses from your garden? They're lovely!'

'I suppose they must be.' Adam frowned at the flowers as though he couldn't think how they came to be there. 'My cleaner must have cut them,' he explained, and Isobel relaxed, glad that Sonia Kenlow wasn't responsible for the roses.

She sipped the coffee, which Adam had laid out on the larger of the tables. She saw with surprise that he had gone to the trouble of preparing a salad, unless the cleaner had left it ready for him, and she realised how hungry she really was. Tired she might be, but she would not say no to that spread. There was ham, cottage cheese, coleslaw and olives as well as the usual lettuce and tomatoes, and she began on the meal, perching a tray on her knees as Adam was doing.

'It was good of you to go to all this trouble, sir,' she told him between mouthfuls. The lettuce was really crisp, and she picked up a leaf and munched it, feeling strangely at home.

'You need feeding up. You're too skinny, young woman,' he said with mock severity, and she smiled, wondering if he ever said that to Sonia Kenlow, who was even thinner.

She concentrated on her salad after that, but still managed to eye him covertly when he was similarly engaged. He wasn't quite as handsome as Paul. His features, though handsome, were not regular, his mouth was a fraction too wide, the chin too determined—the chin of a man who always got his own way. She liked his straight nose, though, and the way the cleft in his chin deepened in anger or amusement. In no way did he compare with the leanly athletic Paul Ashe, naturally. He was much older, too, perhaps bordering on forty, she reflected, then cast the idea hurriedly away as he seemed to become aware of her scrutiny.

Those deep grey, almost black eyes settled upon her face for an instant and she took her time cutting up a tomato, hoping he hadn't misconstrued her interest. She was simply making a general comparison between him and Paul, that was all.

The consultant was too old, too worldly-wise. He needed the Sonia Kenlows of this world, the sophisticated elegant women who knew the ropes. What he did not need was a frigid girl of twenty-three, however suitable she might be in other ways. Adam Sheridan should have a warm wife, someone to whom he could turn on cold winter's nights. A woman who would offer him every creature comfort, not flinch away because her precious virginity was more important to her than the man in her life.

She sat up, that new thought disturbing her. If she had refused Paul it must be because she didn't love him enough. She tried to conjure up his face as she finished the last of her meal. Yes, there it was—the lean face, the sensuous mouth, the expressive blue, blue eyes. And he was smiling. Somehow those eyes turned to stormy dark grey, though, the sexy mouth widened, became a hard, firm line, and she longed to kiss it, to feel that hard, almost cruel mouth crushing hers.

Horrified, she quickly gathered up the plates, taking Adam's automatically, just as if she was at home and she and friends were sharing a meal and the washing up afterwards. Later, she blushed at her own temerity, but at that moment it seemed perfectly natural.

She stacked the dishes on one of the trays and was about to pick it up when Adam took it from her. 'I'll carry this. We'll leave the plates in the sink—Mrs G. will wash them for me tomorrow,' he assured her.

'Tomorrow is Sunday,' she pointed out, stifling a yawn as her much shorter legs followed him into a big, high-ceilinged kitchen.

'So it is,' he agreed. 'I'd forgotten today wasn't supposed to be a working day. Sonia will wash them—she's coming to lunch tomorrow.'

All the pleasure went out of Isobel's evening and she made no comment as she watched Adam put the dishes in a bowl and run hot water on them. Sonia Kenlow was lunching with him tomorrow. Why not? She was his fiancée, after all. It was a wonder he hadn't spent today with her, come to that. She would not be pleased to wash *two* sets of supper dishes!

'Why isn't she here today?' She blurted out the question unthinkingly, and wished it withdrawn the moment it was out. 'She called on the ward this morning and asked where you were.'

'Did she?' The bushy, expressive brows met in a frown. The frown was directed at Isobel herself, she felt sure, not at Sonia Kenlow. 'She telephoned me here just after lunch. I'd been out looking at some properties.'

'Oh? Are you moving, then?' Perhaps Miss Kenlow didn't want to live so far from town.

'No. I like it here.' He hesitated, then went on: 'I'm trying to find a suitable property for MS patients—and others, perhaps. Somewhere people like Mrs Chipchase could go, be looked after if they need it, yet a Home where they could keep their independence for as long as possible.'

Thrilled, Isobel encouraged him to go on. She hadn't known he cared so deeply. She could forgive him a lot if he truly cared about the forgotten people like Mrs Chipchase. That he took a keen interest in multiple sclerosis she already knew, after the short but enthralling lecture he had given the Bladen Ward staff earlier in the week.

'Nothing suitable has turned up so far. Then there's the question of money. I shall need money—plenty of it. Something that's in short supply,' he added ruefully, and Isobel nodded.

'Something will turn up, I'm sure of that,' she insisted.

'Something has. Miss Kenlow has a suitable house and she's willing to turn it into such a Home if she can get planning permission.'

Coldness touched her spine. 'I'm glad. Will there be a place for Mrs Chipchase?' If her favourite patient could be settled then she would be overjoyed.

'I expect so. It all depends. Mrs Chipchase hasn't that long to live—I'm sure you realise that?'

For some reason, she hadn't. Oh, she knew at the back of her mind that there wasn't going to be any remission for the woman now. Yet there was always hope. 'I suppose I *did* know, but . . .' Her voice trailed away as she turned from him, forlornly. Poor Mrs Chipchase! Poor Adam Sheridan, too. Now she could see why he was engaged to such a totally unsuitable woman. He needed Sonia Kenlow's house.

Tears welled up, a combination of sorrow and sheer exhaustion. Whether they were tears for herself or Mrs Chipchase or for Adam, she could not have said. Angrily she wiped them away, fishing for her hankie in her uniform pocket. For once she was glad of the Highcastle uniform dress, with its capacious pockets.

With her hankie she pulled out the sheet of

notepaper on which Paul had written his address in
Newcastle and the telephone number.

Hastily she blew her nose. Adam picked up the
sheet of paper, his eyes on her. 'I'm sorry,' she
muttered. 'I expect it's tiredness.'

If she hoped for a comforting shoulder to cry on,
she was disappointed.

'It's after eleven, young woman. I'd better take
you home.' His voice was sharp, disapproving.

'Thank you, Doctor. I . . .' She took the sheet of
paper he offered, guilt overcoming her when she
saw Paul's handwriting—light, sharp strokes of the
pen, typical of his mercurial personality. He would
be worried. No, the night nurse would tell him she
had left with Dr Sheridan. But the night nurse
would expect Dr Sheridan to return home while she
went to her quarters in the Nurses' Home. No one
would imagine that the haughty consultant had
taken a mere staff nurse home to supper!

'A friend from London?' His tone was sharp.

'He . . . he called on the ward today. He came up
unexpectedly, and I arranged to see him after
duty.' She hated having to tell him, somehow she
felt the knowledge of a man in her life must be kept
from him, but that was a ridiculous idea.

'He'll be put out when he knows you preferred
my company,' he remarked. 'Get your cape and I'll
run you back. Or I'll drop you in the town, if you
prefer?'

'No, thanks. I want to get into bed as soon as
possible!' she laughed shakily, then flushed as he
raised a brow.

'Lucky man,' he commented, and she wanted to
hit him.

'No!' she protested. 'It isn't like that—he's just a friend. I'm tired!' she wailed, feeling those stupid tears coming back. Adam was always a trying person, but tonight he was particularly so, and she wouldn't care if she never saw him again.

Wordlessly, he held out his arms, those strong, welcoming arms, and Isobel went into his embrace, forgetting how trying he was! There was no hesitation on her part. She didn't love him; she didn't even like him. Yet she needed the comfort only he could provide.

He let her cry into the softness of his suit jacket. It smelled deliciously male, and she snuggled closer, feeling safe and secure. With a small sigh she allowed her tired eyes to close, enjoying the strength of his arms around her, the satisfyingly broad chest on which she rested.

She felt his lips in her hair, heard him whisper her name. Bella—how beautiful it sounded! The merest whisper, his use of the name a caress.

Imperceptibly, his arms tightened and she snuggled into him. When his lips descended upon hers she was ready. Her lips met his without surprise. She had wondered how that cruel mouth would feel if ever he kissed her, and now she knew. The kiss rocked her to her very foundations.

Unable to bear the ecstasy, the fire that raged throughout her body, she tried to pull away, to free her mouth from the savage onslaught, but in vain. Then, when his mouth finally left hers, Adam trailed kisses down her cheeks, her throat, and she moaned. The passion he aroused in her was almost too painful to bear. At that moment she could have denied him nothing.

It was Adam who finally ended the embrace. His hands settled just under her small breasts and she flinched at the touch of his fingers, suddenly afraid, remembering Paul's clumsy caresses. He must have felt or heard the frightened thudding of her heart, because he let his hands drop to the curve of her slim hips. Then he released her.

'I'd better get you back to the hospital. Your friend will be worried.' The deep voice was shaky for once, unsure, and her heart went out to him. She had an overwhelming urge to offer him comfort, just as he had offered her, but the face he turned towards her was the face of a stranger, a weary stranger. His expression was cold, distant, the grey eyes dark with pain.

'I apologise, Nurse Ford,' he said formally, while inwardly she cried. 'Put my inexplicable behaviour down to the weather. Too much sun isn't good for any of us.' He turned away, picking up his car keys from the table.

Without a word Isobel gathered her cloak about her and followed him from the house. In those few precious moments she had learned one thing about herself: whatever difficulty stood in the way of loving Paul as she ought to, it certainly wasn't frigidity. Her entire body was afire, lit by the flame from Adam Sheridan, a man who meant nothing to her.

In her whole life she had never known emotion such as the one which swept through her now. She yearned for more, complete fulfilment. Adam Sheridan had lit a flame and she didn't know how to douse it. Even the love of her life, Paul Ashe, hadn't managed to turn her bones to jelly and her blood to hot, fiery lava. She had thought of herself as an iceberg, but now she knew the truth. She was a volcano—a dissatisfied volcano. Adam Sheridan had brought her to the edge of the crater and then left her there. Her hunger had gone unassuaged, and she faintly resented it. If only she hadn't flinched just then! If only she could have responded to him the way a warm-blooded, experienced woman would have. If only . . .

'Perhaps you'll give me a rundown of the patients, Isobel.' Sister Sowerby's face was vibrant and alive, love emanating from every pore, and Isobel smiled.

The tall, elegant Evelyn Sowerby was in love. Her engagement ring, a sapphire, was suspended on a chain which she had hidden under her starched navy blue uniform. She had been a widow for several years and Isobel was delighted at the unexpected announcement. Sister was to marry an engineer some time before Christmas. She would, Isobel thought, have made a far more suitable wife for Adam Sheridan than Sonia Kenlow.

She mentioned Adam's engagement, just to see her senior's reaction. Surprise crossed Sister Sowerby's face, then she made a moue. 'So! She's cornered him at last!'

'You know her, then?'

'Yes. She and Adam Sheridan have been going around for a couple of years, I should think. High time he married her!' she laughed, her tone implying that the couple were lovers and that marriage was only a formality for them. 'There used to be a rumour going around that I fancied him, you know,' she went on.

'I wondered about that,' said Isobel. 'You'd make a better wife for him than that woman!'

Evelyn Sowerby eyed her shrewdly, and Isobel realised she had spoken too vehemently. She didn't know why she disliked Sonia Kenlow. The woman had done her no harm, she mustn't be so bitchy about her.

'I think coupling my name with Adam was wishful thinking on the part of the hospital grapevine! It was more *because* of my name, really. Adam and Evelyn,' Sister explained, seeing Isobel's blank expression.

Of course—Adam and Eve. How suitable that sounded!

'I've known him for years,' Sister went on. 'Has he found a property yet? He's looking for a place for MS patients.'

'I know,' Isobel affirmed. 'He told me last night.'

'Oh?' There was a wealth of meaning in that one word, and Isobel felt awkward. Dr Sheridan wouldn't want anyone to know she had spent part of yesterday evening with him.

'He told me when . . . when he was here. He helped with the emergency,' she hurried on.

'Ah yes, Mrs Dean. She's making good progress. That's a relief. Now,' Sister said briskly, 'who is who and what have they got? I know most of them, of course.'

'Mrs Dean was new. And we've had three discharges,' Isobel explained. 'Oh, Mrs Dailey is back, to give her daughter a rest.' She flicked through the card index. 'The only patient you don't know is Mrs O'Brien. She's got leukaemia,' she said. 'There doesn't seem to be anything we can do for her.'

'There's always something we can do, Isobel,' Evelyn Sowerby said decisively. 'Even if it's only to make them comfortable towards the closing of their days, it's something. Never forget that.'

'No, Sister,' she said meekly. Sister was right. That was what made nursing such a pleasure even when a lay person would seek in vain for something pleasant about the work. A warm glow within her, she accompanied Sister Sowerby on the rounds. Nursing was wholly satisfying and there was nothing else she would rather do.

Last night she had spent in foolish dreams, yearning for a tall, dark, broad-shouldered man whose face was hidden from her. She had been pursuing him and every time she caught up with him he had the smiling face of Paul Ashe. Yet she knew it wasn't Paul for whom she hungered. She was longing for a man she didn't love and couldn't have, anyway.

She smiled at old Mrs Dailey. Nursing and the patients were the only important things in life. Men, she could do without. Particularly the consultant physician!

CHAPTER FIVE

ISOBEL was off duty at two on Sunday, and she eyed the rain clouds as she hurried back to her flat to change. After days of drought and the sunniest weather imaginable it was back to 'outlook unsettled', as the weather forecasters termed it.

Paul was picking her up about three, so she had just enough time to make herself a sandwich, then shower and change. He . . .

The subject of her thoughts grinned lazily at her from the doorway of the Nurses' Home. Without hesitation she accepted his kiss, a mere brushing of lips. She was glad it wasn't more passionate than that. She didn't feel in the slightest bit passionate; all she wanted was a shower, then a long sleep. She wished, too late, that she had been firmer with Paul on the telephone last night, but it was no use regretting her acquiescence now.

'I'll come up while you change. Here—I got you a salad roll.'

'Oh, thanks! I haven't eaten since breakfast. Though Sister let me go for a coffee break this morning.' Heart thudding, Isobel led the way up one flight of steps, then along a short corridor to her flatlet. She didn't fancy entertaining the hot-blooded registrar on her own, but she could hardly leave him outside.

'Here we are,' she said brightly. 'Home, sweet home.'

Here we are—home at last. Adam Sheridan's words of the previous evening came flooding back to torment her, and she barely listened as Paul chatted away about her old hospital, telling her about people she knew, places they had visited together.

She made him a cup of coffee and produced sweet biscuits, the sort he liked.

'Just like old times, Isobel.' His expressive eyes searched her face as if seeking reassurance, and she smiled at him.

He appeared ill at ease—that was probably why he was talking so much. Maybe he wondered what her feelings were towards him now. She didn't bear him any resentment, not now. The hurt, the pain of rejection, the bewilderment, all were in the past.

She studied him covertly while he drank his coffee. He was just as handsome as she remembered. Just as smart, too. The lightweight grey suit fitted as though it was tailor-made for him. But he lacked Adam Sheridan's rugged masculinity. Ashamed of her train of thought, Isobel swiftly asked after Paul's parents.

'They're fine. Dad's retiring next year, and they may sell the house and move to Spain. I'll keep the flat on there until it's sold.'

Paul had a top floor flat in his parents' house. It was there that he had tried to make passionate love to her, and hastily she put the thought aside. There was no point in digging up the past; the whole embarrassing episode was better forgotten.

Paul, it seemed, did not want to forget it. 'About last time we met . . . I'm sorry for what I said, Isobel. Truly.' His innocent gaze held hers and, impulsively, she leaned forward and squeezed his hand.

'I didn't take it to heart—really, Paul,' she assured him, overwhelmed at the unexpected apology. 'I understood that it was your hurt pride talking,' she added, and a look of astonishment crossed his face.

'It was not! My pride wasn't hurt at all! I was concerned for you, that's all.'

Now he was annoyed with her. She'd said the wrong thing again, been tactless. Rather like her relationship with Adam Sheridan, she thought wryly. Whatever she said or did, it was usually wrong. She blinked, certain she had seen Adam sitting beside Paul. Oh, go away! she cried silently. Leave me in peace, can't you!

'Isobel? Are you OK?' Paul moved from the settee and perched on the arm of her chair, and she tensed, hoping there wasn't going to be a romantic interlude. His hand dropped to her hair, then slid down her face. His fingers idly caressed her neck, and she relaxed. What was so terrible about Paul anyway? He wouldn't hurt her. She ought to be more relaxed with men. They weren't all waiting to leap upon her!

'You've changed, Isobel,' he murmured, holding her closer. 'You aren't so . . . so unyielding.'

'I haven't changed that much,' she said evenly, knowing it was a lie. She *had* changed, but only since last night.

'We could stay in,' he suggested, but she shook her head.

'I'll show you some of the beauties of Northumberland,' she offered instead.

'Are there any beauties of Northumberland? Apart from girls, I mean?'

'You'd be surprised, Paul!' Southerners never thought of Northumberland as beautiful, unspoilt countryside, but that was what it was, largely. The industries of the Newcastle conurbation were confined to the south-east corner. Even the Tyne wasn't entirely industrialised. 'There's Hadrian's Wall, but you need sunshine to really . . .'

He snorted. 'Hadrian's Wall? Honestly, Isobel! I didn't come for a history lesson. I came to see you—the girl I love,' he added simply.

Isobel didn't know what to say. Here it was—a declaration of love for which, a year ago, she would have given a fortune. Now . . . Now she wasn't sure. She smiled ruefully. 'Let's keep it light, shall we?'

She saw by his amazed expression that her reply had shaken him. He needn't think he had only to hold out his arms and she would fall into them like a lovesick teenager. In those twelve months she had matured. True, she had spent much of the time pining for the charming, handsome Dr Paul Ashe. Now, her dreams were answered and she wasn't as thrilled as she should have been. She had grown up. She was also wondering why it had taken a whole year for him to realise how much he needed her. She rather imagined the torrid romance he'd been enjoying when she left London had now burnt out, but she didn't pursue the point, not wanting to hurt him. 'Cheer up, Paul. The world hasn't crumbled.'

'Mine has,' he said shakily, but he was soon his usual confident self. When he rested his arm across her shoulders she made no objection. She didn't want anything to spoil their afternoon together.

Rain began to fall as they left, not the soft rain of the south but a cold rain which hurled itself against them, whipped up by the strengthening breeze.

Paul shivered. 'So much for sitting on Hadrian's Wall!' he joked, and Isobel laughed with him.

'We'll find somewhere. There's lots to see—really.'

'Have you adopted the wild northland, then?' he asked once they were on their way. His metallic blue Rover ate the miles and she begged him to slow down. It was Sunday, after all, and only the tourists hurried on Sundays.

She considered his question as he reluctantly slowed down. 'Yes, I suppose I have. Apart from the occasional visitor, all my patients have been Northumbrian. They're very friendly.'

'Not too friendly, I trust? No dynamic Geordie consultants sweeping you off your tiny feet?'

She glanced at him sharply. 'We have two—one's in his late thirties, I should think. The other one is younger,' she went on, thinking of Adam's colleague.

'Oh?'

When she didn't respond, he went on, irritably: 'What about him? This younger one, I mean.'

Mischief lit her gaze. 'He's very nice. Very friendly.'

'How friendly?' demanded Paul, his face getting red, and she dared tease him no longer.

'He's happily married. With four children,' she added truthfully.

'You might have said. I was getting jealous,' he admitted.

Isobel wondered why he didn't question her about the more senior consultant. He would, if he'd seen Adam Sheridan!

'Oh, there's a darling little village coming up soon! You have to turn off at the crossroads.' She navigated for him, consulting a map because she was still unsure of the way. She had a little car of her own but hadn't done much exploring since Sadie left. Now, with summer bursting out all over, she intended to see what she could of the county. She did not, after all, know how long she would be remaining in the north of England. London's call was sometimes very strong. Eventually she would return home.

Home. Her home was wherever she happened to be. Apart from a few friends at the London hospital where she had trained, she had no ties in the capital. There was no reason why she could not live in the north or anywhere else, for the rest of her life. No reason except Paul Ashe.

They stopped in the little village street. It was no longer raining, and a watery sun was shining fitfully. Everywhere was quiet after the bustle of the morning. The pretty little church slept, the only sign of life anywhere being a black cat which sat in a nearby doorway, cleaning its fur.

Isobel got out to stretch her legs, a reluctant Paul following. 'This is one of the prettiest villages in this area, Paul. It's a pity it isn't sunnier. Perhaps we . . .' She stopped in confusion. How could they come again? Tomorrow Paul would be returning home, speeding down the motorway, 'leaving

Northumberland—and Isobel—far behind.

He had already spent almost a week in Newcastle attending a medical conference. Isobel had imagined his visit to her was to relieve the monotony of the weekend, and his declaration of love had thrown her. She wasn't sure she believed in him any more. In her own mind she was convinced that, once he returned to the bright lights of London, she would not see him again.

Paul began to grumble, turning up his coat collar. 'It's cold, Isobel. Is there somewhere in Newcastle we could go?'

'It isn't cold!' she protested. 'The wind's a bit fresh, that's all.' She gazed about her, willing him to see the beauty of the hamlet. It was set in a sheltered valley, and she could just make out the thin ribbon of water that wended its way towards the sea, many miles distant. The church nestled in the centre of the village, mature trees affording plenty of shade. More clusters of houses lay to the west, while to the east gently wooded hills rose, stretching away as far as the eye could see. Each house had a neat fenced garden, set out dolls' house fashion, and Isobel longed to walk up a path and knock on someone's door.

The clouds eased away and the sun shone down again, sunlight catching the stained glass window of the church, reflecting back diamonds of colour. She stood enthralled, the sheer beauty piercing her heart. She swung round, eager to share the moment with Paul, but he was halfway back to the car and with a shrug she followed him.

When she suggested they might try to find some of the many castles in the area or visit Hexham

Abbey, he looked astounded, and she said no more.

In the end they dined at a neon-lit club in the heart of the city, the noise blasting Isobel's nerves after the tranquillity of the countryside. When Paul yelled across that it was just like being in London, she agreed with him.

There was a dance-floor to one side and she went into his arms eagerly, hoping to recapture some of the magic they had known before. It was a modern dance and most of the couples were dancing slightly apart, jerking in time to the music, but a few were dancing cheek-to-cheek like Isobel and Paul.

'This is more like it,' he murmured against her hair. 'I've been thinking about you a lot lately. Every time I met a redhead I thought about the prim and proper Isobel Ford.' When she would have interrupted, he put his fingers across her mouth. 'No, listen to me, darling. I'm not getting at you. I like the starchy Staff Nurse Ford just the way she is. Could we start again? No strings, no insults. No lovemaking, if that's the way it has to be. Isobel?' His tone was anxious and she hastened to put him out of his misery. Friendship was all she asked of him. She would be desolate if they parted for ever, though it wasn't likely they would meet often, separated as they were by several hundred miles.

'I'd like that, Paul, I really would. Just a friendship,' she said firmly.

If he was disappointed that friendship was all that was on offer, his expression didn't show it. 'Just good friends,' he agreed. When the dance ended, he dropped a chaste kiss on her brow.

After the dinner and dance he drove her back to the hospital, then waited, apparently expecting an invitation up to her flat for coffee.

Knowing Paul as she did, she realised that such an invitation would be unwise. His good intentions might fly out of the window! Instead, she thanked him politely and truthfully for a wonderful evening, and did not draw away when he leaned forward to kiss her. Gently he undid her seat-belt, then wound his arms about her, hugging her to him. With a sigh she snuggled closer, pulling away only when his kisses became demanding.

'Paul! You promised.'

'I know, I know. I'm sorry.' But he didn't sound sorry and she was disappointed in him. Part of the fault was hers for responding, she knew. She must keep him at arm's length.

He was returning to London after lunch the next day and he promised to pop into Bladen Ward to see her before he went. 'To say a second *au revoir*. Don't worry,' he assured her, seeing her unenthusiastic expression, 'I won't get in the way.'

For some reason she wasn't keen to be seen with Paul. Sometimes Adam Sheridan popped in on a Monday and if he saw Paul he would have further reason to dislike her. He wouldn't tolerate a nurse's private life spilling over into duty hours and wouldn't hesitate to say so.

She couldn't stop Paul coming, though, and didn't want to hurt his feelings. After one final attempt to persuade her to offer him coffee, he gave in. Isobel watched his car until it was out of sight. In the darkness, she waited until the tail lights disappeared into the night, wondering why her heart didn't ache at the thought of him leaving tomorrow. Why, she might never see him again! The thought, once faced, was unpalatable.

Confused and weary, she made her way back to the Nurses' Home. Perhaps tomorrow she would see matters more clearly, the problem of Paul being put in perspective after a good night's sleep.

Isobel was on late duty on Monday but arrived well before she was due in case Paul came earlier than planned. She wanted to intercept him, if possible, before he got to the ward office. Sister Sowerby might object to his presence, for one thing. So might Adam Sheridan. She didn't want the two men to meet, being absolutely sure they wouldn't get on. Adam was blunt to the point of rudeness sometimes, and if he wanted Paul off the ward, he would say so without coating his request in polite southern terms!

Sister greeted her with relief. 'What a morning! Dr Sheridan brought two students from Newcastle around, and they questioned every symptom, every little detail. I was that glad to see them go!'

Isobel laughed, but Sister wasn't in a joking mood. 'He's in a mood, Isobel, so watch it. He'll be back later, after his clinic.'

There was no need to ask who 'he' was. Her heart sank. It was going to be a dreadful afternoon.

'New admission coming after lunch, when I'm off,' Sister went on. 'A Mrs Dixon—Susie Dixon. Early sixties. Congestive cardiac failure, poor kidney function as well. It's just for a checkover more than anything. She's been chronic for several years.' Sister handed Isobel the case notes. Already the notes were bulky, and she sighed.

'Quite a bit of reading there, so get stuck in. Oh, there was a phone message for you, a young man who seemed to think you'd be on duty.'

Sister eyed her speculatively, and Isobel tried to look nonchalant. 'It was Dr Ashe, I expect. He's an old friend—well, a colleague, really. He's from London.'

'I hope he isn't trying to get you back to the bright lights, Isobel. I'd miss you. You've fitted in well,' Sister added, and Isobel's heart glowed.

'Have I really? I . . . I wonder sometimes. I mean, me being a southerner and all.'

'A nurse is a nurse no matter where she comes from,' Evelyn Sowerby said firmly. 'Good nurses aren't that plentiful, and you're a good nurse. I know at least *one* consultant who thinks so!'

Isobel thought for one wonderful moment that Sister meant Adam Sheridan but, of course, that was foolish. He didn't consider her to be a good nurse. He barely tolerated her, and certainly would not sing her praises to the Ward Sister.

Later in the afternoon, she sat with the new patient for a few moments. Student Nurse Ruddock and part-time Staff Nurse Shafto had admitted Mrs Dixon and made her comfortable. Isobel had seen the husband, a burly miner, whose taciturn manner and blunt Tyneside speech were a little off-putting at first. Yet the man cared deeply for his chronically sick wife, and Isobel felt she had left him sufficiently reassured. The woman was in no immediate danger; she was simply on the ward as a precautionary measure and for observation.

She was a poor colour and rather breathless after the exertion of being put to bed, and Isobel gently smoothed back the patient's iron-grey hair, which was damp with perspiration. David Hanington hovered at her elbow before she could do more than ask Mrs Dixon how she was feeling. She let Staff Nurse Shafto attend him, and walked slowly back to her office. Paul's message had said he would be leaving later than planned and would call in during the nurses' tea breaks.

Isobel glanced down at her fob watch. Not long till teatime. Even as she thought that, the ward doors swung open and the domestic assistant wheeled the ladies' tea-trolley through. Isobel sent Student Nurse Ruddock to help give out the tea and cake, where appropriate, then tensed, feeling dark flinty grey eyes boring into her back. She knew it was him even before she spun round, her face flushed.

Adam Sheridan stood in the doorway of Sister's office, one big square hand resting on the door frame. Isobel felt her colour deepen and her heart-beat increase. It was ridiculous the effect he had on her. The worst of it was, she didn't know *why*. If it was Paul she could understand it. Perplexed and annoyed both with herself and Adam Sheridan, she greeted him coolly. 'Good afternoon, sir. Mrs Dixon has just arrived. Dr Hanington is with her now.'

'I'm surprised you aren't assisting him, Staff Nurse.' His tone was equally cool, and she remembered Sister's words about him being in a mood.

'Staff Nurse Shafto is attending him, Doctor,' she said firmly, her hackles rising at the implied criticism. When Sister was off duty *she* was in charge and could not be expected to undertake every nursing chore herself. 'She's a very good nurse,' she added huffily, just to drive home the point, and his eyes glinted.

'I've no doubt she is!' he snapped. 'I've had one hell of a day, and I don't want to bandy words with you, young woman. I'll take a look at those.' He picked up the case notes and sat down behind Sister's desk, leaving Isobel quietly fuming. She clenched her fists, wishing she had the courage to slap his proud, arrogant face!

Then her temper subsided. If he was having a bad day she mustn't add to his troubles. He had no right to take it out on her—but that, she reflected wryly, was what nurses were for. It was the consultant's privilege to wipe the floor with them occasionally and she must grin and bear it. Yet how different was Paul Ashe! He was always unfailingly polite to nurses of all grades and his charming smile and devilish grin had all the females, patients as well as staff, eating out of his hand.

This irritable, proud Northman was his exact opposite. Personable he might be when he chose and with the charisma that high office brought, but he was nonetheless chauvinistic, arrogant, rude, pigheaded . . . She paused in her silent inventory, because the boyishly handsome figure of Paul Ashe stood in the doorway, surveying the scene with a big grin.

Horrified, Isobel put her fingers to her lips, but Adam Sheridan had already seen the newcomer. It was too late. Paul was caught in the laser beam of Adam Sheridan's gaze.

'Yes?' he barked, and Paul's grin slipped. He glanced uncertainly at Isobel, who shook her head.

'I'll see you outside the office,' she murmured, almost pushing him out. She closed the office door behind her, leaving Adam Sheridan to his work. 'I thought there was going to be bloodshed then!' She managed a shaky laugh, and Paul raised his brows.

'Is that the older consultant you spoke of?' His eyes searched her face as though he suspected her of lying.

She nodded. 'He's in a foul mood for some reason,' she whispered. 'I go in fear of my life when he's like this!' She tried to make a joke of it, but Paul did not appear to see the joke.

'You told me he was old!' he hissed, and she began indignantly to deny it.

'No. I said he was in his late thirties and that he's older than the other consultant. He's not some greybeard, silly!'

'He's not what I expected, either.' Paul's tone was sulky. 'I imagined a bald head and glasses, or something.'

Isobel's finely marked brows arched and her eyes flashed in temper. She wasn't a redhead for nothing! 'It isn't my fault you suffer from an over-active imagination!'

'The bloke's handsome,' he muttered, then shot a dazzling smile at Aimee Ruddock as she passed. The student blushed and giggled, which did nothing for Isobel's temper.

'If you've come to say cheerio, then say it, Paul. I have plenty to do and there's a woman-eating doctor in the office, don't forget!'

'I don't eat women on Mondays,' a chilly voice

put in, and Isobel spun round, her heart descending to her sensible shoes. Neither of them had heard the door open and the consultant must have been very quiet. Furtive, she thought, with a return of the anger. He'd been eavesdropping!

'I . . . I'm sorry we disturbed you, Doctor,' she said hastily, letting her eyes show the anger her tongue dared not speak. Briefly she introduced the two men. Adam Sheridan's nod was curt.

'I hope you haven't come to lure Staff Nurse back to the bright lights of London,' he said irritably, his brows drawing together in an ominous frown.

Paul's polite smile wavered. 'I wish Nurse Ford had never left, sir. She's needed at her old hospital.'

'By whom, I wonder?' was the icy rejoinder, and Isobel longed to shake the man. He was being deliberately rude, trying to provoke Paul for some reason.

Paul seemed to be struggling to find the right words, and she knew he would never back-answer a consultant; he had great respect for rank. 'Well—to be honest, I need her, sir. Nurse Ford and I were very good friends.'

Isobel closed her eyes in horror, but Dr Sheridan made no further comment, beyond asking, very politely, if Staff Nurse could spare him a few moments.

Paul squeezed her hand, then, with a cheery wave, was gone, leaving a shaken Isobel to follow Adam Sheridan into the office.

'You wanted me, sir?' Her voice trembled and she strove for control.

His smile was enigmatic. 'Hardly,' he said dryly.

'Ah, yes—Mrs Dixon. She's an old hand. I've seen her a lot at OP, but she's rarely admitted. Hospitals give her the screaming habdabs, so be gentle with her.'

Stung at his first remark about not wanting her, she was further incensed by his advice to be gentle with Mrs Dixon. As if any of the nurses would be cruel to the woman! 'We are *always* gentle with the patients, Dr Sheridan.'

His eyes were on the notes again as if what she had to say was of no importance. So, after a momentary hesitation, Isobel gathered her courage for a final onslaught. He was too arrogant, too fond of treating her as a serf. And his remark implied a criticism of the nurses as well as herself and was totally unjustified.

If she'd been calmer to begin with, if Paul hadn't appeared at the wrong moment and upset her equilibrium, she wouldn't have been so foolish as to clash with the consultant. As it was, training and common sense flew out of the window. 'I regard your remark as a criticism of myself and my nurses,' she carried on, talking to his dark head, for he still didn't bother to glance up. 'A totally unjustified criticism,' she finished, trying to keep the quiver from her voice. She was beginning to realise what she had done. Provoked the woman-hating doctor to heaven knew what retribution! He might insist upon her being moved! She couldn't bear that.

He was busily writing, but at length he glanced up. 'I'll take a look at the woman once David's finished.' He was, apparently, going to ignore her outburst and she didn't know whether to be pleased or sorry! That her opinion was of no consequence,

he was making abundantly clear. It would be better
if she said no more and hoped they might get back
to their old footing—coldness on his part, cool
efficiency and politeness on hers.

Yet she felt she must apologise. She hadn't been
rude, but the man was tired and out of sorts,
anyway. 'I'm sorry, sir,' she said stiffly, resentment
stirring in her breast.

'Are you, Bella?' His use of her name threw her,
then she smiled.

'No, not really,' she admitted, and he chuckled.
She watched in amazement as his grey eyes lit up
with laughter. He looked years younger as he
laughed, and she joined in, half in amusement, half
in some unexplained emotion.

Suddenly she knew it to be sadness, yet there was
no reason for her to be sad. She hadn't angered
Adam Sheridan after all, so she wouldn't have to
leave Bladen Ward. It must be because Paul was
going home, back to London, back to her old
hospital, taking his friendship and his declaration
of love with him.

Her smile was wistful as she took the case notes
from Adam. His gaze was intense, those beautiful
dark eyes flint-hard no longer, and her breath
caught in her throat. She knew now why she was
sad.

CHAPTER SIX

ADAM SHERIDAN'S round day. Sister Sowerby normally accompanied him, but she had an emergency dental appointment, so it fell to Isobel to stand in for her superior. Heart thudding, she accompanied him on his round of the patients. He stayed longest with Mrs Chipchase, and told the patient that there was at last a vacancy for her.

Mrs Chipchase eased her tormented body in the bed and Isobel was immediately at her side, plumping up the pillows. She and Nurse Ruddock helped her to sit up again.

'Next week some time, I should think,' Adam went on quietly, and Mrs Chipchase clasped his hand, her eyes brimming with tears.

Isobel, too, was near to tears as they finished the round. She and Adam Sheridan strolled companionably back to the office. Her mind was on Mrs Chipchase and the unexpected vacancy, but also on Sonia Kenlow. Now Adam might not have to marry the woman just to provide a home for Mrs Chipchase. The thought delighted her now that she realised the awful truth—that she loved the fault-finding Adam Sheridan!

Once back in Sister's office, the companionable mood vanished and his eyes were bleak, chilly, as she questioned him about Mrs Chipchase. 'It isn't the vacancy you thought you might have, then? You told Mrs Chipchase that something might be

81

going to turn up. And I wondered . . .'

'You think I have an inexhaustible supply of places for the chronically ill?' he suggested, and she flushed.

'No, of course not, sir, but you told Mrs Chipchase that there could be a vacancy somewhere else!' she insisted.

'That won't be just yet!' he snapped. 'Be thankful her name has come up at all!' He turned away as if to leave the office and Isobel wondered how—and why—she had come to love this irascible, complicated man. She must be out of her mind and ought to be admitted to the psychiatric unit as soon as possible!

As though relenting, he came back. 'The other vacancy, the Home, depends upon Miss Kenlow. My fiancée . . .' He paused, and Isobel found herself nodding in understanding.

'You told me she has a suitable property. Is it all arranged?' She was surprised at the calmness of her voice.

He ruffled his thick, dark hair, leaving it more unruly than ever. It made him look curiously vulnerable—younger, too, and her heart swelled with love for him. 'Permission has been given—in outline, anyway. I keep looking for somewhere else, perhaps nearer town, but . . .' He made a helpless gesture.

He seemed surprised when she asked him why he took such an interest in multiple sclerosis patients. 'Because of my father. He had a stroke and died soon after it, but he had some of the multiple sclerotic symptoms. Luckily he died before the disease became progressive.'

Her eyes darkened with sadness, as she said: 'It doesn't always become progressive, though, does it? Sometimes it can remain steady.' She was thinking of Avril as she said that.

He nodded curtly. His eyes narrowed as they rested on her flushed face. 'You seem to take a special interest in MS, too. Or am I mistaken?'

Glad that he was at last interested in her viewpoint, Isobel went on to explain about her friend. 'She still gets about. It's only sometimes she has to use a wheelchair. Usually she gets about with a stick or holding on to furniture.'

'You keep in touch?' he wanted to know.

'Yes, in a way. Once she had to discontinue training she shut herself off from the rest of her set, but I tried to keep in touch with her. Now she writes sometimes, or her auntie does. When I go back to London I'll pop in to see her. I often used to phone her.' She paused, feeling guilty because she hadn't telephoned recently. She nibbled her lower lip, making a vow that she would ring Avril that very evening.

Abruptly he changed the subject. 'I suppose you'll be going back to London quite soon?'

Surprised, she blurted out: 'Of course not! I expect I'll drop in when I get my holiday.'

'Oh? Seeing your *friend*, I imagined you would be following him shortly.'

She didn't like the way he emphasised the word 'friend'. 'You mean Dr Ashe? He just popped in to see me while he happened to be in the area. He . . . We were only—'

'Spare me the biological details!' he snarled, and they glared at each other.

Really, he was the most impossible man! If he wasn't engaged to be married she might even believe him to be jealous of the younger, more personable man. The whole thing was ridiculous. If David Hanington hadn't returned then, heaven knows what she might have said to Adam Sheridan!

She was off duty at five and thankfully left the ward. It was another hot and sticky day and she hurried up to the flatlet, keen to strip off and shower. After that she didn't know what she would do. She had no plans for what remained of the afternoon, though about nine o'clock there was to be another party in the common room and she intended dropping in. Most of the time since coming up north she had been busily nursing her broken heart and feeling miserable. All for nothing, she realised now. She still loved Paul in a way, but it was nothing compared with the emotion that surged through her whenever she met the dishy Dr Sheridan.

After her shower she shampooed her hair, then wrapped herself in a towelling robe and settled down to read. Late afternoon sunlight streamed into the room and she got up to open another window. It was hotter than ever, stifling, and she reckoned a thunderstorm could not be far away. She had lovely views from the flatlet, though some people might not have thought so as it overlooked the hospital campus. True, she would have preferred a window overlooking a real old English country garden rather like Adam's, perhaps, but she could see plenty of life from her window.

Down below nurses and other staff scurried to and fro. Most of the office workers had left, but a few stragglers were making their way to the car park, over to her left, or to the bus stop which was out of her line of vision.

She spotted the physiotherapist, then one or two of the domestic staff she knew. Adam Sheridan's secretary was making her way to her sports car, then she waved to someone, and Isobel leaned farther out of the window, trying not to expose too much bathrobe-covered body. Her eyes followed the secretary's gaze and she found herself looking at Adam Sheridan. His determined stride was unmistakable, and he was heading straight for the Nurses' Home!

Hastily she drew back. He could not, of course, be calling on her. Or could he? Was it some emergency on the ward? Why should he want her if it was?

Questions without answers hurtled through her mind, and she was taken aback when there was a confident knock at her door. It must be one of the girls; it couldn't be him. She stared down in dismay at the rather short robe she wore, then shrugged. At least if it was Adam it gave her an excuse for not letting him in. It wouldn't be professional.

She inched the door open, peering round it so that only one arm and part of her right shoulder were visible.

The fine grey eyes betrayed no emotion, not even surprise. 'Am I disturbing you, Staff Nurse?' His tone of voice was formal, distant, and Isobel shook her head, wishing she hadn't been so lazy. She ought to have dressed straight after the shower. She could, at the very least, have dried her hair; now it lay in soft damp curls against her scalp.

'No—that is, I've just had a shower. I'm sorry I can't ask you in,' she mumbled, thinking it was just as well that she couldn't.

'I suggest you put on something more substantial, *then* ask me in. I can hardly stand in the doorway!'

She had irritated him again. That wasn't difficult. 'Yes, of course, sir. I'll not be long.' Hastily she shut the door in his face, then realised how rude that seemed—just as if he was a door-to-door salesman whom she didn't trust! Feeling foolish, she re-opened it and quickly invited him in.

His expression was astonished, as well it might be, and she flushed under his gaze. 'That was a quick change of clothing,' he commented, stepping across the threshold.

Scarlet-faced, she muttered something unintelligible, then fled to the tiny bedroom in search of clothes. She put on a cool cotton dress of blue with a design of small white daisies. She knew how well blue suited her and it was her favourite dress. Hastily she partly dried her hair, then made her way back to the sitting room where Adam Sheridan was standing by the window.

He turned as if sensing her presence, then his gaze dropped to her feet and she realised with horror that she was still barefoot!

Unwilling to search for her slippers, she perched on the edge of the two-seater settee, realising too late that he might get the wrong idea and think she wanted him to sit beside her. Quickly she rose before he could move from his position by the window, and joined him there. She pretended an interest in the goings-on below while she waited for her face and body to cool. What a fool he must think her!

'You're an extraordinary little thing, Nurse Ford.' He sounded faintly amused, but she chose to believe that his humour was patronising.

'I suppose it's because I come from London!' she snapped. 'Probably northern nurses aren't extraordinary in the sense *you* mean!' Immediately she was contrite, the more so because he didn't retaliate, merely sighed heavily.

'I'm sorry, Doctor, you must think me very silly.' It took all her courage to say that, and she was near to tears. Why, oh, why did she always have to spoil things between them? If she was to have a chance with him she must become cool, sophisticated, elegant . . .

She nearly laughed outright. Staff Nurse Ford was anything but sophisticated and elegant. It was too, too ludicrous. Then she thought she had better wipe the smile off her face. Adam Sheridan looked far from amused.

'I really came about Mrs Bland.' He spoke into the taut silence.

'Is that your friend who suffers from multiple sclerosis?'

'Yes, that's the one. She asked me to look out for a nurse for her and I thought of you.'

To say she was surprised was putting it mildly. 'Me? I thought you didn't like me!' she blurted out.

'Sometimes I do, sometimes I don't,' he said gruffly, leaving her as perplexed as before. 'When you explained your interest in the disease I realised you might do for Mrs Bland—though she needs a companion more than a nurse. The disease is fairly stable at present.'

'I don't know what to say.' And she didn't. She doubted if she could be of much help to his friend, particularly if the woman didn't need actual nursing. Then there was Highcastle General. If she left there she might never see Adam Sheridan again, or at least not in a medical capacity. It would be painful never to see him; never to bear the brunt of his uncertain temper; never to watch the cold flint-grey eyes darken with rare amusement or with tenderness when he was with a patient . . .

'Would I see you there?' The words came out unrehearsed and she coloured deeply. Now she'd thrown herself at his head! Now he must realise how she felt. She didn't know where to put her face, and though she amended the telling sentence and tried to change its meaning, the more she said the deeper she implicated herself.

He listened in apparent amusement. He was laughing at her, and the worst of it was, she deserved it.

Gently he put out a finger and tilted her chin, forcing her to meet his gaze. His eyes were kind, understanding, but she didn't want kindness! She wasn't a child or a kitten whose amusing yet destructive ways had to be tolerated until she reached a certain age.

Exasperated with him, she turned away. 'I'd like to help your Mrs Bland, but I have to stay at the General. I'm sorry.' She was ashamed of her earlier stupidity, and truly sorry that she couldn't help Mrs Bland.

'She lives near the hospital. You could pop in to see her,' he suggested, and she brightened.

'Could I? I'd like that,' she beamed, the green eyes sparkling, and a soft moan escaped him.

'Bella.' Her name was the merest whisper and she wasn't sure she had heard him, wasn't sure he had even spoken, for his mouth closed in a firm line.

She fought down the insane longing to kiss him, try to prise apart those firm, sensual lips. Funny, once she had considered his wide mouth had a cruel set to it. There was nothing cruel about Adam Sheridan—or if there was, she no longer cared. Whatever he did to her she was his, whether he wanted her or not.

As if in a dream she glided towards him, walked into his arms as if it was the most natural action in the world. Or perhaps he walked into *her* arms. She couldn't remember afterwards which it was. About the actual embrace there was no doubt; it was satisfying to them both.

Isobel stood on tiptoe and wound her arms around Adam's neck, pulling his head down nearer her level. His hair felt crisp and satisfying beneath her fingers, and she moaned in ecstasy as his sensual mouth hovered above hers. Then he crushed her slender body to his and she lost all sense of time. It might have been minutes or only seconds before he released her. Her nerve-ends were jumping about all over the place, knocking against one another. Her heart raced away, but erratically so, and she felt most peculiar. She swore she heard bells ringing, but it could have been Adam's heart beating powerfully next to hers.

'I want you, Bella.' The words were softly spoken, but she heard. Want, not love. He couldn't even pretend to her. But at least he wasn't lying. He was speaking the truth, believing at last that she was adult enough to accept it.

Her eyes were two great pools of emerald as she met his gaze. Greatly daring, she ran her fingers down his face, down the intelligent brow, the straight nose, the wide mouth. They settled on the cleft in his stubborn chin and gently she caressed it. That he wanted her was obvious, and she knew only a supreme effort of will was preventing him from making passionate love to her.

Yet that was what she wanted! She loved this coldly controlled man, this arrogant, demanding chief, this wonderful physician. And he was promised to another woman, so she could never have his love, enjoy it by right. Whatever he could offer her she would take gladly, humbly. Her expression must have told him that, for he closed his eyes momentarily, and when he opened them again they were full of pain. 'Forget me, Bella,' he said quietly.

Before her startled senses could react, could demand that he stay on his own terms, he grasped both her hands in his and pressed them to his lips. Then he left.

Numbly Isobel watched the door close behind the love of her life. I want you, Bella, but forget me . . . The words echoed and re-echoed in her tired brain. Her past failures crowded in on her, Paul's insistence that she was frigid, unable to love. Now, when she thought she had broken free and had offered her love, she had been rejected.

She might be a good nurse, but she was a failure as a woman. Even the man who professed to want' her had been able to walk away.

Dry-eyed, she sat staring into space until dusk fell.

CHAPTER SEVEN

ON Friday, Paul telephoned Isobel on the ward. It was in the middle of the morning rush and Paul really should have known better.

As luck would have it, Adam Sheridan walked into the office as Isobel was patiently trying to explain to Paul that she couldn't talk to him now as they were so busy.

Sister Sowerby intercepted the consultant and firmly backed him out of the door, to Isobel's great astonishment. Ward Sisters had wonderful powers of persuasion! As they left she heard Sister telling him that it was Nurse Ford's boy-friend on the telephone and that they mustn't stand in the way of young love.

That was all Isobel needed! Her face burned as she finally persuaded Paul that he must ring her at the Home. She would stay in tonight and expect him to telephone. He started to tell her some news, but crossly broke off when she explained that the 'older consultant' was hovering outside.

The line crackled with his anger. 'He *isn't* older, Isobel! He's just your sort!'

Annoyed with him, she replaced the receiver. Paul was right, though she doubted if he realised it. Adam Sheridan *was* just her sort. The man himself didn't know, that was the trouble!

As soon as she replaced the receiver Adam walked in. If she hadn't known better she might have believed he'd been listening.

'Can we resume our work now?' His tone was cold, the dark grey eyes glacial, if it was possible for dark eyes to be glacial! 'We are paid to work,' he emphasised, settling himself in the visitor's chair and eyeing Isobel.

Her smile was taut, controlled, but smile she did, even though she wanted to shake the man. Can't you see what you're doing to me! she wanted to shout. Can't you see I love you?

But of course he chose not to see. He was going to marry Sonia Kenlow, for better, for worse. Perhaps he didn't realise it was for worse. Maybe he actually *loved* the woman.

That was a new and unpalatable thought, and Isobel's eyes widened in dismay. All along she had assumed that he was simply making use of Miss Kenlow, that his main interest was in the use of her home for his multiple sclerosis patients. Now she took a closer look at the idea it seemed ridiculous. It was, at the very least, unworthy of him. He must really care for her. After all, even Sister Sowerby had hinted that it was high time he married Sonia.

She gazed at him with new insight, then hastily buried her face in Mrs Dixon's case notes. She had been about to write a short note about the woman when Paul phoned.

'Will you have dinner with me tonight?'

Wondering if she'd heard right, Isobel looked up in surprise. Was that invitation for her?

The faintest of smiles crossed the firm mouth. 'Yes or no?' Adam enquired mildly.

She floundered for an instant. Here she'd been convincing herself that he loved Sonia Kenlow after all, now he wanted *her* to dine with him! Why?

Her eyes asked the question, and he shrugged. He was about to speak, but Sister hovered in the doorway. Behind her Isobel saw Mrs Dixon's husband, and the moment for explanation passed.

Mrs Chipchase was due to be moved some time the following week, and Isobel took a few minutes off from her other duties to speak to her. She did her best to sound cheerful, wondering all the while how long Mrs Chipchase would survive.

'Shall we get you up for a little while, Mrs Chipchase? Sister said you weren't feeling too grand, but—'

'If you could help me further up in the bed that will do. I don't want to sit out today.'

'You had a few minutes out when they made your bed, so perhaps that's sufficient for today,' Isobel agreed, wondering why the normally cheerful patient wore such a sad expression.

Isobel and SEN Mackenzie settled her more comfortably. When she and the patient were alone again, Mrs Chipchase burst out: 'I don't want to go!'

'Go where? To the Home? You'll be better looked after there.'

'I won't! I won't!' To Isobel's consternation the woman burst into tears.

'Mrs Chipchase!' she scolded. 'We can't have tears. You'll like it there, I know you will.' She cradled the tear-stained face against her shoulder, sending up a hopeful prayer that she was right. The Home would have a better staff-patient ratio and they would be skilled in the care of the handicapped. They would have more experience in caring for the terminally ill, she felt. The move was for the best.

When Mrs Chipchase was calmer, Isobel left and made her sad way back to the office. Perhaps if Adam hurried and married Sonia that house would be available and Mrs Chipchase could go there.

She accepted that even if the work was started straight away it would take time—more time, perhaps, than Mrs Chipchase had left. She bit back a tear, feeling foolish. It was unprofessional to cry. She was behaving like a fool; she wasn't usually so emotional. Adam Sheridan was the cause. It was all his fault!

Before she knew it, she was back at the office where the aforesaid Adam Sheridan and the Ward Sister were deep in conversation. They didn't notice her. The doctor was forcefully making a point and Isobel turned hurriedly away, not wanting to butt in if he was in another mood.

Then she heard her name and she swung around in astonishment. They were discussing her!

'I want Staff Nurse Ford and I shall have her!' His tone was determined, and Isobel's mind went winging back to that wonderful moment when he told her: 'I want you, Bella.' Now he was telling Sister Sowerby! Her brain accepted that it wasn't the same kind of wanting, naturally, but it brought back a memory she was trying hard to bury.

'You can't!' Sister Sowerby's voice broke in on Isobel's thoughts. 'She's needed here. With respect, Adam . . .' Here Sister took a deep breath and Isobel knew that Adam was about to be soundly ticked off! Sister was the only person who could handle him, and Isobel wished she could become invisible so that she could pick up a few tips!

Then they saw her and Sister beckoned. 'I've been telling Dr Sheridan that you can't leave us. He's wanting a nurse for a friend of his.'

'Yes, I know, Sister,' Isobel agreed unhappily.

'You might have told me.' Sister's voice was reproachful, and Isobel flushed.

She started to explain that she had never had any intention of leaving, when the consultant broke in: 'It may have slipped her mind, Eve. I'm sure she meant to tell you.'

Isobel gasped at the unfairness of it all. 'I didn't! I never meant to—' she began, but irritably Adam waved her to silence.

'You can give in formal notice now and then leave at the back end of next month.' His tone was firm. The great man had made the decision and there could be no argument.

She opened her mouth to protest, nevertheless, but this time it was Sister who crossly waved her away. 'If you've made up your mind, Isobel, there's no point in my trying to persuade Dr Sheridan. Now, there's a Miss Dodd coming in this afternoon.' She handed over the case notes and Isobel stared at them blankly. She didn't *want* to go!

She flicked through the notes. Another diabetic woman for stabilisation—only this one was blind.

'Memory impairment,' Adam put in, and Isobel raised her green eyes to his.

'I beg your pardon?' She couldn't absorb any new information just yet. She was to leave the hospital, leave Bladen Ward simply to nurse a woman who was in a state of remission anyway. She could not. She . . .

'I said Miss Dodd has an impaired memory,' he said sharply, and she nodded, the mists clearing. Miss Dodd's bed must be prepared; nothing else mattered.

Miss Dodd was clearly disorientated. Being blind didn't help, either. Then there was the diabetes. She was in her sixties but looked older. She had a bright smile for everyone and Isobel knew she would quickly become a favourite with nurses and patients alike.

It seemed a shame to put her to bed in the middle of a sunny afternoon, but Isobel assured her it was only until the doctor had examined her. 'Then you can sit in a chair if Doctor says you may.'

'I should like that, Nurse dear.' She put out a fleshy hand and Isobel gripped it. Miss Dodd was terribly overweight and a strict diet would have to be enforced. She had a feeling that it wouldn't be easy.

She was right. Later, when she was writing the report, the third-year Nurse Peters handed her a bag of chocolate biscuits and assorted toffees that she had removed from Miss Dodd's locker. 'Her nephew must have brought them in. They weren't in her case.' Nurse Peters dumped the offending objects on a chair, and Isobel surveyed them gloomily.

'Has she eaten any?'

'She says not, but she probably can't remember. I lectured her about sticking to a diet and when I told her she mustn't eat toffees, she sounded surprised. 'Oh, mustn't I, Nurse?' Nurse Peters gave a passable imitation of Miss Dodd's gravelly voice, and Isobel smiled wryly.

'Her memory cells are so few that she probably *was* surprised when you told her that. She obviously doesn't remember what she can and can't eat.'

Another problem to add to all the others. Yet wasn't that what nursing was all about? She settled down again to the report, only to be interrupted some moments later by the nursing auxiliary, Mrs Richards.

'It's Miss Dodd, Staff Nurse. She's gone a funny colour!'

Isobel hurried to Miss Dodd's bed, which was nearest the office. The woman was lying back, her face putty-coloured. Isobel bent over her, then Miss Dodd struggled up, smiling. 'Just taking a little nap, dear. Is it teatime yet?'

There were sighs of relief all round, and Isobel checked Miss Dodd's pulse while Mrs Richards explained that tea *and* supper were finished.

'Do you feel all right, Miss Dodd? No dizziness or headache?' Isobel asked.

Miss Dodd announced that she felt fine, but wanted her tea!

'God love her,' murmured Mrs Richards. 'Isn't she a flower, then!' Her broad Geordie brogue was music to Isobel's ears, and she laughed.

'Yes, she *is* a flower, Mrs Richards.' Still smiling, Isobel made her way back to the office. She would call the duty doctor just to be on the safe side. Apart from the diabetes, Miss Dodd's heart was taking a tremendous strain with all that extra weight; she really was colossal.

These were the people Adam Sheridan wanted her to leave, but there was no way that she would.

Isobel stepped wearily under the shower and washed away the cares of the day. She was late finishing because of staff holidays and it was nearly eight before she left Bladen Ward, her duty really finishing at five.

Revived by the shower, she slowly dried and dressed. As she wasn't going out she didn't bother too much. The pink and white striped dress was old and comfortable. It needed sewing, she found to her annoyance.

Sighing, she took it off again and sat in her bra and panties while she mended a small tear under one arm. There was no hurry to dress; she wouldn't be called to the telephone yet awhile. That thought had no sooner left her mind than there was a knock at the door. She hesitated. It might be Paul ringing early, or—or it could be dear Dr Sheridan. She hadn't forgotten the surprising invitation to dinner, of course, but she thought it had probably slipped his mind. If he wanted to talk about Mrs Bland he could do so on the ward; he need not go to the trouble and expense of inviting her to dine with him.

The knock came again, impatient, demanding. That was definitely Adam Sheridan!

Her heart racing, Isobel quickly slipped the dress over her head, then opened the door—to find the tall figure of David Hanington.

Taken aback, she murmured a polite invitation and he walked in, grinning. 'You need to button up that dress, Isobel. I can see all you've got!' he quipped, and a horrified Isobel hastily did up her top button.

Her fingers were fumbling with the next button when a cold voice interposed: 'I can see all she's got, as well!' Adam Sheridan strode in after David, closing the door behind him.

Stupefied, Isobel could only stand and stare as the consultant frowned at his registrar. 'Are you a friend of Nurse Ford?' Adam's tone was ominous, and Isobel felt for David. He was visibly squirming under his senior's steely gaze.

'Why, aye! All three of us are, sir. Me and Lynne and Isobel,' he floundered on.

'Oh?'

'Well, I'll be getting back, then.' David gave them both a sickly grin, but Isobel put out a detaining hand.

'You haven't told me what you wanted, David.' Her tone was gentle. The poor man had forgotten what he'd come for! Rather like Miss Dodd and her useless brain cells.

'Oh aye! Yes, it's about supper on Sunday. That'll be fine, thanks.' With an audible sigh of relief David Hanington made his escape, leaving Isobel to do battle with the suspicious-minded Adam.

'What was that about supper, Bella?'

'He's coming to supper on Sunday, Doctor,' Isobel said, stubbornness preventing her from adding that his wife would be coming as well.

An angry frown marred his features, and, relenting, Isobel was about to explain about Lynne when he snapped: 'Aren't you ready yet? I've booked a table.'

Hands on hips, she eyed him defiantly. All the while her pulses were racing away and she knew quite well that she *would* dine with him. No way was she turning down the invitation! Then she remembered Paul. He would expect her to be there when he phoned!

Her face clouded and she shook her red mop of curls at Adam. His eyes roved briefly over her abundant hair, then dropped to her partially-unbuttoned dress. 'Are you wearing that for dinner?' he asked, temporarily throwing her.

'No, of course not! It's old!' she protested, anxious to get rid of him before her blood pressure shot up to an unacceptable level!

'In that case I'll resist the temptation to button you up. I'll wait while you change.' Glancing about for a chair, he settled himself finally on the settee.

A whiff of aggressively male aftershave drifted across to her and her mind noted that it was different from his usual one before she recalled herself to the task in hand: explaining to the masterful doctor that she could not dine with him.

'I'm very sorry, sir,' she began, 'but I'm not free this evening.' There, let him make of that what he would. For heaven's sake, he was an engaged man! He had no right to take out other women. But she wasn't, of course. She was only Staff Nurse Ford, who had to be persuaded to bend to the consultant's will and agree to nurse his friend. Apart from that she was of no interest to him.

He rose quickly and Isobel backed away from his anger. He gripped her slender wrist, his fingers like a vice, and she cried out in pain. 'Why aren't you free?' he demanded, pulling her against him.

She felt the expensive cloth of his dark suit against her cheek as she was held effortlessly. 'I'm waiting for a phone call. From my boy-friend!' she flung at him.

Abruptly Adam released her, his mouth set in the grim lines she knew so well. 'The man I love,' she added for good measure, wishing she could break his heart as he was breaking hers. She rubbed her wrist, the mark of his fingers still visible. 'You hurt me,' she muttered, but if she hoped for sympathy she got none.

He ran his fingers through his unruly hair, leaving a strand of hair over his right eye.

Her fingers itched to push it back for him. They itched, as well, to muss his hair a little more. The very few strands of silver at his temples were more visible this evening, or so it seemed. He wore his age proudly, like a badge. He was an experienced physician, a highly-qualified doctor; he was entitled to a few grey hairs. To her they added to his appeal, lent him a distinguished elder statesman air, but he misconstrued her look, because he said, savagely: 'I'll be thirty-nine next birthday. Quite a greybeard, aren't I!' He flung the words at her, his face bitter, and she found herself shaking her head.

'No, no, you're not!' she cried, hurt because he was hurt. 'I . . .' Just in time she stopped herself blurting out the awful truth—that she loved him. 'I'll get ready,' she said instead, and hurried through to the bedroom, closing the door firmly behind her.

She agonised over what to wear and finally decided on the pearl-grey suit. With it she wore a pink silk blouse. Redheads shouldn't wear pink, or so she'd been told. Yet it lent colour to the suit and she thought it blended nicely with her hair—she hoped it did, anyway. She wasn't a mirror-gazer and there was no vanity in her, yet as she checked her outfit in front of the full-length mirror she couldn't help wondering if the dynamic consultant found her attractive.

Later, as she sipped her Martini in the under-stated luxury of a country hotel, she knew the answer to that question. Whenever she had dined with Paul Ashe his eyes were never far from hers. He gave her his close attention, to the exclusion of everyone else. The distinguished consultant thought it unnecessary. She was only a nurse, she reflected without bitterness. He wanted to tell her about Mrs Bland, that was all.

He was politely attentive, though. His manners were impeccable when he chose to exert himself. She had the feeling that he was miles away, though, and she tried hard to steer him back. She glanced about her, seeking for a topic of conversation, some item on which she could comment. The hotel was old, parts of it dating back to the sixteenth century, though much careful restoration had been done. Low beams in the alcove had caused the tall doctor to bend his head. Even Isobel found the ceilings low, the dining-room small. Yet it was cosy and felt homely, and she commented on its olde-worlde atmosphere.

Their eyes met. His were grave, watchful, and she blushed, without quite knowing why. 'History has always interested me,' she hurried on, to cover her confusion. 'It was the only subject I liked at school, apart from literature,' she laughed. 'And biology, naturally,' she added truthfully. The workings of the human body had always fascinated her, and when career-choosing time came it was a difficult decision to make—should she go into nursing which was always her first choice, or ought she to stay on and perhaps take a degree, turn her interest towards some form of research? She was glad now she had come out in favour of nursing and had never regretted it. She didn't enjoy studying and knew she might not have gained that vital higher qualification.

'Naturally.' His voice was curt, and she looked her surprise. Her thoughts had been winging back to the past, yet the past contained Paul Ashe, not this man.

'Naturally you would prefer biology,' Adam added, seeing that she wasn't completely with him. 'Women invariably do,' he added dryly, and her eyes flashed, but she refrained from comment. No good would come from antagonising the man.

Instead she said: 'Tell me about Mrs Bland. Is she still in remission?' Her tone was cool, and amusement lurked in his grey eyes.

The waiter hovered then. When they had chosen, Adam explained about his friend. 'She was a friend of my brother's, actually. I have an older brother in Canada. He and June were in love at one time. If there is such a thing,' he added, and Isobel was astonished at the bitterness in his voice.

'June Bland is in her late forties and she's had multiple sclerosis for years,' he went on, his tone carefully neutral again. 'She has spent time in a wheelchair, not because she really needed one but because it was easier than managing crutches or hanging on to furniture. She's had the house adapted to her own needs. You'll like it there. It's not too far from the town, but it's within reach of some breathtaking scenery.'

Their first course, melon, was placed before them, and silence reigned as they began on the meal. How could she possibly leave the hospital? All her patients, the staff, people of whom she'd grown fond.

It was on the tip of her tongue to regretfully refuse, but when she pushed the empty dish aside she found Adam's eyes resting on her, those fine grey eyes almost willing her to accept, and she wavered.

She was still wrestling with her decision when the main course arrived. Her steak looked and smelled appetising, but she couldn't bring herself to begin on it until the important matter of her future had been decided. She was needed at Highcastle General. Was she needed at Mrs Bland's?

'Please help June. She needs you, Bella.'

It was as if he'd read her mind. Yet still she persisted: 'The patients need me too, Doctor.'

'There are other good staff nurses in the vicinity. Anyone with the right qualifications and manner can do your work at the General. It takes a special person to help someone like Mrs Bland—a person like you.'

He didn't beg, he didn't plead. Yet his eyes, his whole body, was willing her to accept. A special person like you.

You are special too, Dr Sheridan, she wanted to announce to anyone who would listen. There was a warm glow within her as she agreed. For Adam Sheridan's sake as much as the patient's, she would try to help her.

CHAPTER EIGHT

ISOBEL met Mrs Bland the next day. Adam picked
her up bright and early that morning as she was off
duty all day. She had mixed feelings as she sank into
the leather upholstery of his car. For one thing, she
wondered how she and Mrs Bland would get on.
For another, it was bad for her blood pressure
and her heart having to sit next to the dishy Dr
Sheridan! Particularly as he spent the short
journey talking about his fiancée, she might have
added.

'Sonia prefers city life, but I love the countryside,' he began as he guided the car skilfully out
through the one-way system of Hardcastle.

Isobel smiled wanly but said nothing. It was
only natural that he should want to talk about
the woman he loved. She now accepted the fact
that he must love Sonia Kenlow, and it hurt like
hell.

'Tired, Bella?' He shot her a brief, concerned
glance and she nodded.

'Yes, I am rather. I didn't sleep too well, Doctor,' she admitted. She had been sleeping badly
ever since she realised she loved the man. He was
entirely to blame!

'Call me Adam as we're off duty,' he invited, to
her secret delight. Adam Sheridan—Adam. Adam
and Eve. If her second name was Eve that would be
just perfect. But it wasn't, it was Margaret!

'Sonia's there.' Her Adam broke into her thoughts of Paradise.

'Where? With Mrs Bland?' She didn't need his quick nod; she had already answered her own question. Sonia is there. But why not? It was natural enough, particularly if the two women wanted to discuss the projected conversion of Miss Kenlow's house into a Home.

The sparkle went from the day, even though the sun was already hot. She was pleased that she was wearing her new dress, a soft floaty fabric in various shades of green. She hoped Mrs Bland wasn't superstitious!

Despite her day being spoiled by another woman's presence, it wasn't all minus. Apart from that one brief conversation on the ward, she hadn't met Sonia Kenlow. She was curious, keen to see more of the elegant Miss Kenlow.

Miss Kenlow was waiting at the door of Mrs Bland's house. There was no sign of Mrs Bland and Isobel's first impressions of the house were of an old, rather gloomy building, creeper-strewn and in need of repair. A more romantic person would have called it a house of character, a suitable setting, perhaps, for a Brontë novel.

'Darling Adam!' Sonia Kenlow's voice was light and melodious—rather pleasant, Isobel conceded, more so than her own brisk, nurse-like tones, she felt.

Adam Sheridan drew her forward and introduced them properly, since they had met so briefly before, and he stood a little way back as he did so as if to compare the two of them.

If he was making a comparison Isobel knew she

would come off worst. Love was blind, but in any case, Sonia Kenlow was beautiful, startlingly so. Her blue, blue eyes surveyed Isobel without welcome, but without suspicion or jealousy. To her Isobel Ford was just another nurse, a rather lower form of life, apparently, than she was used to.

Isobel shook the delicately-boned white hand with its blood-red polished nails, and couldn't help wishing she could grow her nails to that length. Nursing was hard on the nails as well as the hands! It wouldn't do to go on duty with such talons, which could cause a nasty scratch, particularly where patients like Mrs Chipchase were concerned.

Sonia led the way with Isobel following and Adam bringing up the rear. He was close behind her and she could feel his warm breath on the back of her neck.

Mrs June Bland was a tall, elegant woman, with the air of a grande dame, and Isobel's smile faltered. No way could she be a nurse to someone so grand. She simply would not fit in, and it would be best to tell Adam on the journey home. Yet the woman's smile held the warmth Sonia's lacked, temporarily erasing the lines of suffering which marred her handsome features.

A patient was a patient, no matter how grand, how wealthy, and Isobel's heart went out to her. Perhaps nursing her would not be very different from nursing Mrs Chipchase, except for the degree of disability involved.

They sat companionably drinking coffee on the terrace—Isobel and Mrs Bland having a businesslike discussion of signs and symptoms, while Adam and Sonia sat close by but enjoying their own conversation.

'I've had multiple sclerosis since I was twenty-three,' Mrs Bland explained.

'Dr Sheridan said you were having a period of remission now. How long has it lasted?' Isobel wanted to know.

'Oh, about six months, I should say. Time for a relapse, I expect,' the older woman said wryly. There was no trace of self-pity in her voice, and Isobel often found this in the severely handicapped or very ill patient. Mrs Bland accepted her disabilities when they came and enjoyed her surprisingly frequent periods of remission. She wasn't, she explained, confined to a wheelchair; she could get about, but with some difficulty. The chair was useful when she was feeling particularly tired. 'Or when I can't be bothered to struggle around with a stick,' she smiled. 'I abhor crutches. They aren't the easiest of aids to manipulate, but on the whole my arms aren't affected. It's the legs mainly.'

'June's tongue isn't weak, though,' Adam put in. 'She keeps that well exercised. Don't you, my friend!'

Adam Sheridan and June Bland exchanged secret smiles and there was obvious affection between them, as between nephew and aunt perhaps. 'I enjoy good conversation,' Mrs Bland admitted, then went on to question Isobel about her tastes in music and literature. When she found that Isobel enjoyed a good play, she was overjoyed.

'How very charming!' trilled Sonia Kenlow,

making Isobel feel that a love of drama was a fault to be corrected!

She wasn't sorry when the time came to leave. Mrs Bland extended a lunch invitation to them all, but Adam couldn't stay and the two women left with him. Mrs Bland had a live-in housekeeper, so she wasn't entirely alone. She extracted a promise from Isobel that she would call again soon. 'So we can have a nice private chat,' she said amiably, as first Sonia and then Adam kissed her cheek. Isobel could hardly follow suit on so short an acquaintance, so she shook hands with the woman instead.

She felt a warmness emanating from June Bland and knew that once the initial strangeness had passed, they would get along splendidly.

The following week passed swiftly, Isobel handing in her notice on the Friday. She could leave at the end of July. On the Friday she gazed about her when she got back to the flatlet. She would miss the place. She'd been lucky to have the flatlet to herself once Sadie left. Fortunately most of the trained nurses were married and lived out. She would miss all the company, the freedom that living in the Home gave her. In another year she had intended to apply for a Junior Sister's post at Highcastle or perhaps at one of the Newcastle hospitals, though she preferred the country areas.

Well, that would have to go by the board for now. And if she wanted the countryside she would get plenty of that at Mrs Bland's. Although it was not far from Highcastle, wooded undulating hills enclosed the property on three sides while on the

fourth there were fields as far as the eye could see.
Isobel supposed Mrs Bland owned the fields and let
them to a farmer, for she had seen sheep all around
them. This was a familiar sight in Northumberland,
and Isobel sometimes felt there were more sheep
than humans!

She loved the moorland and the hills, the miles
of quiet, winding country roads. Except for the
heavily industralised area around Newcastle the
county was sparsely populated. She loved the
people, too—one in particular. They *were* different; Adam had joked about it on the way to Mrs
Bland's. Risking a quick glance at him, Isobel had
sensed some of that fierce pride, the aggression of
the northern tribes who had held at bay the might of
Rome.

A tremor shot through her slender body now as
she recalled the conversation. But the drive back
on the Saturday was something she preferred to
forget. Naturally she had quietly got into the back
of the car, leaving the seat next to Adam free for his
fiancée. Sonia Kenlow talked solidly all the way
back to the hospital, and it was a tribute to Adam's
love that he didn't tell her to be quiet, though
Isobel wished he would, however politely he might
express it.

Sonia had excluded Isobel from the conversation, but Adam addressed one or two noncommittal remarks to her and she had answered as
briefly as possible, not wanting to break into their
private discussion.

It was as they dropped her that Adam's remark
caused Sonia's china blue eyes to widen in disbelief.
Her small red mouth hung open for a second until

she controlled herself, and Isobel could understand how surprised the woman must be.

Isobel, replying to some remark of Adam's, had called him 'Doctor'. He smilingly reminded her that it was 'Adam' off duty, and it was that which surprised, even shocked Sonia Kenlow. Isobel heard her complain even before the car moved off.

'Really, Adam, she's only a nurse!' Sonia hissed. 'You mustn't lead her to—' Then the car was moving and Isobel waved to them both, wishing she'd been out of earshot before that remark was made. Sonia Kenlow might prove a bad enemy.

Feeling sad now, she decided that country air would be the best prescription. It was a lovely afternoon and she hurriedly changed into jeans and thin sweater. She would allow herself an hour and see how far she got.

The town had a pretty though small park, filled with flowering shrubs and blossoms of all kinds, and she strolled through there first. Office workers were doing likewise, making the most of a few minutes' respite, perhaps, before they wended their way back to work. In one corner near the lake was a kiddies' playground, and idly Isobel watched the toddlers playing on the swings or digging energetically in the big sandpit—a popular attraction.

A hedge of flowering honeysuckle caught her eye and she went across to inhale its fragrance, so evocative of an English summer. It did nothing to assuage her sadness; indeed, it made her feel homesick. Her heart swelled with a strange longing, but it wasn't for the bright city lights or for the leanly handsome Paul Ashe. It was for Adam Sheridan she yearned.

She glanced back at the children before moving on to watch the ducks diving for scraps. One little boy caught her eye, mainly because he had a mop of black hair, one tendril of which would not be restrained and kept getting into his eyes.

Her lips twitched. Rather like Adam Sheridan! He was getting angry now, with his little fair-haired companion. The fair boy wore a sunhat, and Isobel watched in amusement as Junior Adam snatched the hat and clamped it firmly on his own head. Still smiling, she had just turned her attention to the quaint ducks when there was a scream and she whirled around. Her anxious gaze took in the play-corner, the little fair boy and . . . It was the dark boy. A tall woman had picked him up and he was crying almost silently against her chest.

Isobel hurried across, anxious to help if she possibly could. All sorts of likely occurrences crossed her mind. Perhaps he'd had a fit or an asthma attack. Maybe he'd been stung . . .

His mother was crying, as Isobel and several others clustered around. 'What is it? I'm a nurse—can I help?'

Miraculously the small crowd parted as someone took up the cry: 'She's a nurse. Can she help? Move over—she's a nurse!'

Feelings of inadequacy stole over her, but when she saw the blood she became her own brisk self. The child had cut his foot on a piece of glass hidden in the sandpit.

Gently she staunched the flow of blood as best she could, wishing for her first aid kit. She couldn't press on the wound to stop the bleeding because she thought she saw a piece of glass still imbedded in it. At such times it was necessary both to stop the bleeding and to prevent the glass from being pushed farther into the wound. This was achieved by making a ring bandage and placing it over the foreign body, then applying pressure to the ring itself, leaving the glass undisturbed.

It didn't look serious and the blood had almost stopped now, but the child was clearly shocked and the glass needed removing. One of the bystanders offered the use of her car to get the child to A & E, and in the meantime Isobel made use of the boy's cotton T-shirt which she fashioned into a crude ring, then pressed on it with a clean hankie. She was holding the boy's leg higher than his heart at the same time, which helped the blood to clot. All the time the heart was pumping blood around the body it would continue to spill from the wound, small though it was. Another way to stop bleeding, though not always successful, was to apply pressure to one of the pressure points on the body.

It took only minutes to get to Highcastle and Isobel directed the woman to the side entrance near the ambulance bay. All the while she sat beside the boy's mother, who cradled her small son's curly head against her breast, cooing at him and calling him names like 'pet' and 'flower'. Frank was a stoic little chap and when Isobel smiled at him his dimpled face screwed up into the semblance of a smile. Although in pain he wasn't screaming the place down.

Isobel carried him into A & E, then waited outside until he had been attended to. He emerged later, smiling, though his grubby face was tear-streaked.

'There was only a splinter of glass in it, love,' his mother told her. 'Eeh, I'm that glad you were there!' She started to cry, to Isobel's consternation, and she was trying to calm her when a bigger version of young Frank appeared—Adam Sheridan.

Frank's mother was profuse in her thanks once more, telling Adam that her husband had been laid idle from the Tyne shipyards and that she couldn't take much more. Isobel's eyes darkened with concern, her wistful expression not lost on Adam.

'I suggest we take Frank and his mother for an icecream and then see them safely home,' he commanded, his tone making it more than a suggestion.

Frank's mother gazed at him in admiration as they all sat on a park bench licking icecreams a bit later. Frank was given an especially big ice with a chocolate flake for good measure, and he seemed completely recovered from his ordeal. For being a brave boy, Isobel bought him some sweets, or 'bullets' as he termed them, Adam contributing a toffee apple to be eaten the next day.

They drove mother and son home, and Isobel surveyed Adam once the car was under way. 'It was nice of you to buy Frank an ice,' she said softly.

'And a toffee apple. Don't forget that!' he smiled. 'I should charge you for your icecream,' he added. '*You* weren't a wounded soldier.'

'Mm, you should,' she agreed solemnly. 'I'll buy you one in payment some time, Adam.' She used his name shyly, hesitantly.

'I'll keep you to that.' His smile was warm and she basked in its light.

He offered to drop her off at the park since she had told him she was out to explore, then he said: 'I've a better idea. We'll explore together.' Seeing her astonished expression, he chuckled. 'I could do with the exercise.'

He stopped at his cottage first to change from his formal suit, emerging a little later in jeans and sweater and carrying two anoraks. He offered Isobel one. 'In case it turns chilly.'

Adam parked the car on waste ground well clear of a narrow road which led, he told her, almost to the Cheviot Hills. He got out and pointed. On the skyline she could see the distant hills. In the sunlight a river sparkled, and she knew there were many small rivers in the area. To their left was a wooded valley through which the river ran on its way to the sea.

'There's a bit of drought at present. Not enough to dry up the rivers or cause problems, but it might get worse.' He took her hand companionably as they headed for the valley. Her hand tingled at the touch of his strong, warm fingers, her heart galloping even though her legs maintained a sedate pace.

She was alone with Adam Sheridan. Alone except for the birds wheeling overhead. There wasn't a soul for miles, probably, and certainly no sign of habitation. She trembled at the thought. She and Adam alone. If only . . . If only the shadow of Sonia Kenlow wasn't with them like a cloud blotting out the sun. Still, she must not be greedy. She would enjoy this brief intimacy, this friendship which the consultant was extending. It could not be more than that, for she trusted him completely. If Paul Ashe had her alone miles from civilisation it might be a different story!

Adam stopped and her eyes followed his pointing finger. 'Over there. Can you see it?'

She stood on tiptoe, craning her neck, and he chuckled huskily. 'You'll have to grow, young Bella. Here.' Effortlessly he swung her up into his arms and she stared at him, her face flushed. Then she looked into the distance and saw a ruined barn-type building on a hill.

'That's a pele tower. Most of them are ruined, but some folk have built houses on to them. They were a kind of fortified house where, in the olden days, the cattle could be driven into the lower floor to protect them from cattle thieves and suchlike,' he explained.

'And what happened to the . . .' she began, keen to expand her knowledge, anything to take her mind off his nearness. She had no right to be lying in his arms, and he had no right to cradle her against his chest like this. All thoughts of pele towers vanished when his mouth found hers.

The kiss was long and satisfying, and when Isobel found herself falling she imagined it was sheer emotion. Then she found she had reached ground level again and Adam lowered himself beside her under a great tree whose spreading branches offered a canopy to lovers.

'Bella,' he whispered against her ear, and she squirmed as he nibbled the lobe. 'Delicious,' he murmured, then chuckled wickedly as she pushed him away.

'If you haven't eaten, Adam Sheridan, don't think you're going to dine off me!' She sat up, heart thudding, feeling sure he must see its panic-stricken beat through the thin sweater she wore.

As if by mutual consent they moved into each other's arms again and his kisses became more demanding, seeking from her more than she could give. A picture of Paul floated before her eyes. Then it was the cold blue gaze of Sonia Kenlow she saw, and she began to struggle. Paul was right: she *was* frigid. She could never love a man—

Aware of her reluctance Adam, too, sat up, his eyes dark with desire. 'I'm sorry, Bella, you have an unfortunate effect on me. It won't happen again.'

She pulled down her sweater, crimson with embarrassment. The episode was partly her fault. She must have unknowingly encouraged him—certainly she didn't discourage him. 'You must remember Miss Kenlow—the woman you love,' she faltered.

Silence stretched like an invisible cord between them. 'Yes,' he said finally, getting agilely to his feet and helping her up, his touch impersonal, 'I must remember Miss Kenlow.'

Isobel licked her dry lips, afraid to voice the question but knowing she must, for her own peace of mind. 'Do you love her?'

His eyes were bleak. 'Yes, I love Sonia. Why else would we be marrying at Christmas?'

Why else indeed? The answer gave her no satisfaction, but it was better than not knowing, she conceded. Adam Sheridan was marrying at Christmas. That was that.

Saturday was quiet on the ward and Isobel, who was in charge in the afternoon, was able to get some ward teaching under way. Diabetes seemed the obvious subject since they now had another patient with what was termed 'maturity-onset' diabetes, as well as Miss Dodd. She continued to cause them trouble without realising it. Her nephew was of limited intelligence and didn't seem to realise that Miss Dodd was on a strict diet and could not eat whatever he brought in. She, of course, ate anything she could lay her hands on—crisps being a special favourite of hers.

In vain did Sister and Isobel explain in simple terms that diabetics like Miss Dodd has to eat *some* carbohydrate, but in strictly limited quantities. Everything, Sister had pointed out a few days before, had to be weighed. The nephew's face had cleared and he had nodded vigorously. He would weigh whatever he brought in for his aunt before giving it to her!

This afternoon he had treated Aunt Dorothy to a bag of bananas and two packets of crisps, and only Isobel's vigilance had prevented the woman from tucking into them. Isobel felt sorry for her, but it was useless to explain that all her carbohydrate required weighing and had to be restricted. She simply smiled and said, 'Oh, has it, Nurse? I didn't know,' and like remarks.

Despite her trying ways, the nurses found her enchanting and were reluctant to lose her. She would be going into residential care once her medical condition was satisfactory.

'So,' Isobel began, once the afternoon duties were performed and the visitors were happily

settled at the various bedsides, 'what is the difference between maturity-onset and juvenile
diabetes?' She turned to Aimee Ruddock first, but
it was the new pupil nurse who supplied the answer,
while poor Aimee floundered.

'Apart from the age of onset, the diabetes differs
in severity, please, Staff,' the young girl said
formally. Encouraged to go on, she trotted out a
potted version of Isobel's textbook which she kept
on the ward and let the learners read whenever
possible.

'Yes, that's right,' Isobel approved, wishing
the girl had taken the information and tried to
make it her own rather than mere copycat bor-
rowing. 'The juvenile type needs insulin, but
generally the other type can be controlled by diet
or sometimes by tablets. Now, what about the
tablets? What do they do?' She stopped the pupil
from answering and asked Student Nurse Ruddock
instead. 'It doesn't matter if you don't fully understand, but at least make an attempt, Nurse
Ruddock.'

After one or two abortive attempts, the student
began, then stopped as a man appeared in the
doorway. The little student giggled and Isobel
swung round in annoyance, to find Paul smiling
down at her.

She smiled back, then asked him to explain about
diabetes to her learners. He might as well do something useful while he was here.

She made him feel welcome by the warmth of her
smile, and his blue eyes narrowed speculatively.
Why not? she thought. Paul was once the love of
my life—why can't he be so again? She would do

her best to be a loving girl-friend no matter how difficult that was. Adam Sheridan was lost to her for ever.

CHAPTER NINE

PAUL gave the learners a very brief but concise lecture on diabetes, and Isobel couldn't fault him. His charm was a drawback in one way. Isobel felt that Aimee Ruddock was so mesmerised by his dazzling smile and intensely blue eyes that she gained nothing from the lecture!

When she had dismissed the girls she eyed him shrewdly. 'Not another conference, surely?'

Paul avoided her gaze and smiled brilliantly at a spot just above her head. 'Er—no. No, I came up under my own steam. Of my own free will,' he admitted. 'Just to see my lovely Isobel.'

'Your lovely Isobel wasn't passionate enough for you in London.' If her tone was cynical, he appeared not to notice.

He chuckled. 'I said I was sorry, Isobel. Perhaps it *was* hurt male pride,' he added, to her astonishment. 'You were the first girl who'd ever turned me down, shown a marked immunity to my charms,' he admitted.

'And now there's another girl like that?' she suggested, and knew she had dug out the truth by the way he reddened, though he vehemently denied the charge.

So Paul was using her for reasons of his own, she mused ruefully once he had gone. No doubt he was fond of her and perhaps hoped to lure her into bed, but that wasn't the only reason for trying to rekindle the flame. He wanted his cool girl-friend down in London to know that he was making frequent trips up north to see an old flame. He was using her! Yet her justifiable anger cooled rapidly. Wasn't *she* using *him*? Knowing that Adam Sheridan was lost to her she was turning to Paul Ashe, her second-best love, who would do because there was no one else. Yes, they were both to blame, both being selfish. She could not find it in her heart to condemn Paul. She remained fond of him; if the fondness should turn to something deeper for both of them, so be it. Time would tell. She had between now and Christmas to put the arrogant consultant out of her mind, and Paul's company would help.

He had only the weekend free, his last before his holiday in October.

'Patrick's standing in for me this weekend, then it's back to the grindstone with a vengeance!' he told her over a drink that evening, in a cosy country pub. Isobel had quietly but firmly refused to have dinner with him—why, she wasn't sure. It would be the best way to forget Adam. A meal in an intimate little restaurant in Newcastle, plenty of wine, then a leisurely drive back to her flatlet where they might end the evening in each other's arms. It sounded idyllic, but it wasn't what she wanted. She didn't love Paul, and without love she could not give in to him.

'This is just like old times, Isobel. Why don't you come back to London?' he suggested, with a winning smile.

Isobel was sorely tempted to leave the wilds of Northumbria and return to her home city. It would be so easy. No Adam Sheridan to disturb her thoughts, no untamed, breathtakingly beautiful countryside to tug at her heart-strings . . .

Paul laughed exultantly. 'You're weakening, Isobel!'

'Well—perhaps,' she agreed cautiously, then she remembered Mrs Bland. 'I can't, though. I've arranged to do some private nursing, Paul.' She went on to explain about Mrs Bland, and he seemed surprised that she should leave hospital nursing. Then the peace and tranquillity of the night was shattered when a noisy party of four strolled in, and Isobel and Paul quickly finished their drinks and left.

She breathed in the warm night air as they emerged from the pub. 'It's a beautiful evening,' she remarked, then tensed as Paul's arm snaked about her waist, drawing her to him.

'Relax, Isobel—I shan't bite you.' There was an edge to his voice and she tried to relax, anxious not to hurt him.

When he suggested they finish the evening at her flat she acquiesced. 'A nice cup of coffee is all you're getting,' she warned, but he seemed not to believe her. She wasn't sure she believed it herself.

After the vast open spaces of the countryside, her hospital accommodation felt cramped and confining. She opened the windows, letting in the still warm night air.

Paul yawned, then sat down on the small settee, patting it invitingly. 'Love me, Isobel. Love me.' His voice was soft, sensuous, his smile persuasive, and she did her best to respond to his kisses. Luckily the kettle boiled then and she was able to prise herself free. It was with a sense of relief that she spooned Nescafé into two mugs and poured on the boiling water. She didn't *want* a passionate interlude with Paul—she wanted one with Adam!

She turned, heartbroken. 'Paul—' she began, but he grinned and opened his arms.

Annoyed with herself for not being more positive, she thrust the mug of scalding coffee into his hands, then sat on the only armchair, her eyes dark with unhappiness.

He yelped at the heat of the mug and scowled at her. 'For pity's sake, Isobel! Can't I have a saucer?'

'No, Paul.'

'What?' His expression was astonished, as well it might be. Then he appeared to understand what she meant: no saucer and no lovemaking.

'I'm sorry, I shouldn't have invited you for coffee,' she said miserably.

'Isobel—' he began, then shrugged. 'Maybe I've been pushing my luck. I keep forgetting you're untouched. I don't meet that many virgins,' he added ruefully, and Isobel winced.

'There are more of them than you might imagine,' she said softly. 'All I want—and all I can offer—is friendship. At least for the time being,' she temporised.

'I don't want your friendship!' he exploded. 'I want *you*!'

Her lips tightened. 'It's always what *you* want. What about me? Because I'm only a woman does it mean I get no say in the matter?' she cried. 'What *I* want is friendship. Take it or leave it!' Her tone was firm, and Paul stared at her, his gaze incredulous.

'Isobel, love, this isn't like you . . .' he began, but she cut him short.

'This *is* me!' she snapped. 'I've grown up. I've learned my lesson. No man is worth all the . . . the heartache!' Her voice broke as she thought of the heartache Adam Sheridan was causing her.

Paul left, still angry, and she couldn't blame him.

She lay sleepless that night, the windows open wide to the soft summer air. It was hot, and far away she believed she heard a faint rumble of the threatened thunderstorm. It would clear the air. She wished it would clear away her problems. She wasn't ready for a passionate love affair—but would she *ever* be ready? That was the question that caused her to toss and turn restlessly until morning.

A week of intermittent thunderstorms followed, but Isobel was kept so busy on the ward that the grey, wet weather passed largely unnoticed.

Muriel Chipchase had been moved to a large residential Home miles out in the country, and she kept insisting that she would hate it there.

Isobel was in the office when Sister Sowerby informed the consultant. 'She's probably loving every minute of it now,' he suggested, but Isobel looked unconvinced, and Evelyn Sowerby gave Adam a reproachful look.

'She liked being here, Adam. She was settling in nicely. Some of those institutions aren't all that homely. It isn't as if she'd got a place in the Cheshire Home.'

'No, that's true. I wish I could help her.' Adam sounded weary, and Isobel longed to clasp him in her arms, soothe away the worry lines, kiss away his sorrows . . .

His eyes met hers then, and hurriedly she moved to the Kardex, afraid her thoughts had shown in her expressive face.

'When are you off, Bella?' he asked, and astonished, she swung round, not sure she had heard him right.

Sister Sowerby cast a speculative glance in the consultant's direction but refrained from comment.

'I'm off duty on Thursday, sir,' Isobel answered, her face heated. Calling her 'Bella' in front of the Ward Sister was unwise of him—now Sister Sowerby would wonder.

'Good. Thursday it is, then.' Adam made a note in his diary. 'We'll pop along to see if Mrs Chipchase is settling in. If not, she could go on the waiting list for my own place.'

Isobel heard him with mixed feelings. She wanted to see Mrs Chipchase, and was pleased that Adam hadn't forgotten her, yet it sounded as if Sonia Kenlow's house was almost ready for the first patients. It was full steam ahead once Adam Sheridan got his teeth into a problem, she knew. He steamrollered his way through obstacles with apparent ease, even enjoyment.

On the Thursday it was raining when Isobel awoke, though reasonably warm. She wore her new dress, wanting to look nice for Mrs Chipchase—and for Adam!

She clutched her bag defensively to her as Adam set the car in motion. As well as Mrs Chipchase's favourite magazine she had bought some strawberries and a few useful toilet items for her.

He drove in silence and Isobel didn't known how to break the silence without intruding upon his thoughts. He was probably thinking of Sonia Kenlow, the love of his life, she mused unhappily.

On the road to the Home they passed the spot where Adam had once pointed out the pele tower. And where he had so nearly made love to her. Her eyes darkened with sorrow, a sorrow so great it seemed impossible to bear. Why, oh, why did Adam have to marry Sonia Kenlow?

As if answering her unspoken question, he broke the silence. 'My MS project is getting underway at last,' he said softly, and she murmured some appropriate rejoinder, wondering how far Sonia would allow it to get before the marriage. She felt Miss Kenlow would want Adam's plain gold band on her finger before she let him admit the first residents. She glanced down at her own ringless fingers, and a half-sigh escaped her.

'Why are you unhappy, Bella?' he asked. 'I'm sure Mrs Chipchase is settling in now.'

Relieved that he thought her concern was for the patient, she ventured: 'I expect it was strange for her at first. Have you been to the Home?'

He nodded. 'Only once. It's bigger than the one I'm starting. It's different, too. Basically it's intended for people who are mobile to some degree and who can look after themselves in a sheltered environment. There are almost self-contained bed-sitters with furniture specially adapted to the needs of wheelchair residents,' he went on.

'How will Mrs Chipchase fit in then?' she exclaimed. The bedridden patient could no longer care for herself and she needed constant attention now.

'Don't worry,' he reassured her. 'I'm sure she has

fitted in very well. Wait and see.' A few minutes later they turned in through double wrought-iron gates and Isobel was amazed to see a mansion appear as they negotiated the last bend in the tarmac drive. 'We're here. Now you can see everything for yourself, Bella.' He shot her such a charming smile as he stopped the car that her heart turned over.

He couldn't know the effect it had upon her, otherwise he would have scowled instead! She smiled tremulously, her expressive eyes unable to hide what she felt for him.

The grey eyes deepened to black, and he seemed angry with her. 'Come on, I haven't all day to mess around!' he snapped, getting out and slamming the car door with unnecessary force.

Isobel, hurt, got quickly out without waiting for him to assist her, and glanced up at the impressive building. It was bigger than she had expected and set in beautiful grounds.

'There's a lake over there.' Adam touched her arm to indicate the direction in which she should look, and she flinched, unable to stop herself.

'I'm sorry, I must remember to keep my hands to myself,' he said stiffly, and Isobel was left to follow him unhappily to the open front door. Adam stalked ahead of her, the set of his shoulders indicating his anger.

They were taken to see Mrs Chipchase straight away, and Isobel was amazed to find how much better she appeared. She was sitting up in a chair chatting to another patient, and greeted them with a warm smile.

'Staff Nurse! There was I thinking you'd all

forgotten me!' She hugged Isobel, who had difficulty in holding back her tears.

'There now! Our little nurse takes things too much to heart!' Mrs Chipchase exclaimed, then the consultant had to be hugged in his turn.

The female patients were knitting squares for outsize blankets, and Mrs Chipchase proudly showed off her handiwork, which Isobel duly admired.

Adam prised her away from Mrs Chipchase long enough to show her over the rest of the house. As he had already said, most of the residents were able to manage for themselves and there were three completely self-contained units for wheelchair patients—or 'residents' as Adam insisted they must be called.

Isobel was invited to look around one of the units, and she exclaimed over the beautifully fitted kitchen. All the working surfaces were low, at a height to suit a person working from a wheelchair, and this included the cooker and sink unit. All the rooms were uncluttered, with a minimum of furniture and enough turning space for a wheelchair.

People like Mrs Chipchase were housed in one wing of the mansion. There were three to a bedroom, but the rooms were light and airy and there was ample room for each person to have a few treasures of her own beside her.

Isobel determined to visit the Home again, on her own, and sit with Mrs Chipchase for a while and perhaps help her with her knitting. After coffee with the Matron, they left, Isobel thrilled by what she had seen. If Adam could open a Home like that, somewhat nearer town, it would be ideal;

there was certainly need enough for such an establishment. She was proud of him for making the effort for wanting to do something useful for these people.

'You look brighter than you did on the outward journey,' he commented as they set off for home.

'I'm happy because Mrs Chipchase is settled,' she replied, a little smile hovering about her mouth. 'It's wonderful that you'll be able to set up a Home like that, Adam!'

He chuckled huskily. 'Don't put me on a pedestal, Bella my flower. I haven't started the Home yet!'

She coloured faintly, delighted at being called his 'flower', a term of endearment in the north. If only it were true!

To her surprise he stopped at a country restaurant on the way back. 'It's past my feeding time and I'm hungry even if you're not,' was his reply to her questioning look.

It was bitter-sweet sitting close to him in the restaurant, sipping white wine and listening to the hum of conversation from nearby tables. It was cramped and Adam needed room for his long legs, so Isobel tucked hers under the table while he stretched his out. They were pressed so close together that she could feel the warmth of his thighs against hers—a delicious sensation calculated to take her mind off the food.

So conscious was she of his nearness that she could manage only monosyllabic replies to his questions. It was a relief when the meal arrived. She had chosen a plaice stuffed with mushrooms and prawns while Adam had baked gammon with two poached eggs perched on top. The dishes came with french fries, tiny peas, and loads of salad.

'I can't possibly eat all that,' she protested when the plaice arrived, and he chuckled.

'It will do you good. You need feeding up, Bella. Come on, tuck in, there's a good girl.' She sighed and gave in.

'Thought we'd have dinner in Newcastle,' Adam said conversationally, as they finished their meal.

Isobel paused, the last spoonful of strawberry ice halfway to her mouth. 'Dinner?' she echoed weakly.

The grey eyes narrowed. 'You object to having dinner with me?' he suggested.

Quickly she shook her head. His eyes were on her hair, and she defensively pushed a strand back from her brow. The restaurant lighting was turning the red glints to brilliant burnished copper, and his expression was unfathomable as he said: 'You look like some treasure from El Dorado, Bella. Copper and gold and emeralds—a treasure indeed,' he added softly, and her mouth trembled.

'Don't be so silly,' she said quietly, deeply touched by his remark and trying hard not to show it. 'Anyway, what was that about dinner? I can't expect you to buy me another meal!'

'Why not? It's our day off. Let's enjoy it,' he retorted, his lazy smile warming her.

'What about Sonia?'

His face darkened, and she wished the words unsaid. 'Sonia is in London with a friend. I expect she'll stay there for a few days,' he went on morose-ly, and she believed he was missing his fiancée. It was mean of her to stay away when he needed her to comfort him.

'So you're at a loose end and little Staff Nurse Ford is readily available!' She spoke her dark thoughts aloud, the potent wine causing her unusual outspokenness, and Adam scowled. His brows drew together ominously and she hastily concentrated upon her coffee.

Whatever had made her speak so foolishly? she mused as they left the cosy restaurant. She must keep a careful watch on her tongue in future.

The skies cleared once they were under way again and, when she pressed him, Adam agreed to show her the outside of Sonia's house. This wasn't far from Highcastle, and Isobel was impressed by its beautiful situation. Although not as large as the Home they had just seen, it would hold about eight patients, Adam estimated.

'It has the advantage of being nearer to civilisation as well,' he commented. 'Although it's away from the industrial area around Newcastle, it's within easy reach by car. Pity they closed the railway line, though.'

They smiled into each other's eyes. It was a moment fraught with disaster, for there, right in front of his fiancée's house, Adam took her in his arms. Her lips parted eagerly for his kiss, which was tender, gentle, and brief. She wanted more, and pressed herself against his jacket, seeking the warmth of his muscular chest.

'Bella,' he breathed.

'Adam!' The name was torn from her throat as she clung to him, the tears not far away. She had no right to be in his arms, no right to usurp his fiancée's place, yet she did love him so! Life was too, too, cruel letting her love a man she could not have—a man promised to another woman.

As if drawn by a force stronger than themselves, they came together again, her body melting against his. His kisses became more demanding, his sensitive hands caressing her gently, and she ran her fingers through his untidy dark hair, pulling his head down to her breast.

'Bella, stop that this instant!' he chuckled. 'It's time we left, I think.'

Reluctantly she parted from him, feeling an almost physical pain as she did so. If this was love, you could keep it! She had never felt so miserable in her life.

Although he could not, of course, take her into the house he told her that alterations to the interior would begin soon. Once the workmen started Sonia would move in with her father, who had a flat in the city.

'She wanted to move in with me,' he added, and Isobel bit her lower lip savagely.

'It would be natural,' she muttered, half to herself, and was annoyed when he agreed with her.

She supposed her feelings must be written clearly on her small, freckled face, and she pointedly turned away from him, gazing out at the countryside as they passed.

Endless fields and farmsteads gave way now to woods with tiny streams running alongside the road. In the distance she could see the Cheviots, which were part of the huge National Park.

'How about a visit to the seaside, Bella?' Adam's voice broke into her morose thoughts, and she agreed almost without realising it. She supposed he meant somewhere like South Shields or Whitley Bay. She hadn't yet had a chance to explore the Northumberland coastline, and was pleasantly surprised when they ended up in a tiny fishing village hidden away beside a bay, well off the tourist track.

They got out of the car and strolled companionably by the sea. The breeze was freshening, reminding Isobel that they were gazing out at the unpredictable and often wild North Sea.

She shivered, wishing for a jacket, and Adam draped his own jacket across her shoulders despite her protests. He seemed not to feel the cold, many winters up north having toughened him. She risked a glance at his rugged face as he walked by her side. The wind whipped at his shirt, but he appeared to exult in its power.

'This is the life, Bella. Sun and sea and the wild elements!' he laughed.

'I could do with somewhat tamer elements!' she retorted, eyes shining as she gazed up at her wild northerner. He strode proudly, his face and eyes glowing with the exercise. Then, seeing her face pinched with cold, he put a comforting arm about her and she closed her eyes blissfully for a few seconds. Chilly though it was, this was paradise!

They had early dinner in Newcastle, Isobel finding that the exercise had given a keen edge to her appetite.

While Adam chose the soup of the day, she felt more adventurous and had melon cocktail in port wine. 'I shan't eat a thing all week after this!' she laughed.

'Make the most of it. You can't dine with a consultant *every* week,' he said softly, and her face clouded.

It was only because Sonia was away that she was dining with a consultant now, she recalled, eyes clouded as she began on the first course. Make the most of this meal, Isobel, she told herself. It will be the last time you dine with Adam Sheridan. He belongs in a different world.

Soft rain was falling as they said good night. Adam parked just outside the Home, and she wondered if he would kiss her, wondered if it would be *wise* of him to kiss her. He must have felt the warmth of her response to his earlier caresses; the man should know how she felt!

'It's unfair!' she blurted out as he reached for her hand.

He understood what she meant, for he merely kissed her brow. 'Good night, Bella. And thank you.'

'For what?' she asked. 'I ought to be thanking *you*. For a lovely day and . . . and all that good food . . .' She broke off, willing him to understand the depths of her emotions. When he remained silent she invited him in for coffee, even though they had had coffee at the restaurant.

'If I came in for coffee, Bella, I wouldn't leave till morning.' His tone was husky, seductive.

It was up to her now. If she loved him enough she would willingly give him her love, her all. She knew what she must do, no matter how much she might regret it in the clear light of morning. The words trembled on her lips, but she was given no chance to utter them.

Adam squeezed her hand gently, then was opening the passenger door for her before she was aware that he had moved.

They stood in the light drizzle, two people in a world of their own.

'Good night, Bella. God bless.'

She stood in the doorway of the Nurses' Home and watched him drive away. Then she went up to her flatlet, alone and lonelier than she had ever been before.

CHAPTER TEN

TIME passed swiftly on Bladen Ward after that. Isobel was always a conscientious nurse, but now she threw herself even more wholeheartedly into her work, arriving back at the flatlet mentally and physically exhausted.

She slept soundly at nights now, though occasionally she dreamed of Adam.

Of the consultant himself she saw little, leaving his ward round to Sister or to Staff Nurse Shafto whenever possible. Anne Shafto would be working full-time once Isobel left and there was a junior staff nurse starting in September, so the ward was well covered. Even so, she felt guilty about leaving after so short a time. She was, too, throwing away her chances of promotion.

She visited Mrs Bland once more before she left. Unfortunately Sonia Kenlow was spending a few days there and clearly resented Isobel's visit. Of Paul she saw and heard nothing save one brief telephone call the day before she left, inviting her out to dinner when she was in London. Her acceptance was provisional and guarded. She didn't want to see Paul again. Some memories were better left undisturbed, she realised that now.

She left on a cloud of good wishes, promising to return to see them all. She would be keeping in touch with Joy and with David Hanington and his wife, in any case. They would let her know what

was going on in the ward. It simply wasn't true to
say that nurses forgot their patients the moment
they left a ward for good. Isobel would never forget
Bladen Ward.

On her way down to London for a brief holiday,
she called on Mrs Chipchase and found her
completely bedridden but still active in spirit. She
was thinner, too, but she assured Isobel she was
content.

Seeing Mrs Chipchase reminded her of Adam's
projected Home. Because she had been avoiding
him since that day out, she couldn't ask how the
alterations were coming along. Mrs Bland hadn't
mentioned it, either.

In London she stayed in a small hotel, not wanting to impose on any of her old friends. Avril,
her friend with multiple sclerosis, was much im-
proved and walking well, and Isobel spent most of
her time with Avril and the aunt with whom she
lived.

She did not, after all, visit Paul. That episode was
closed, the wound healed. She learned from a
nursing friend that Paul's romance with a young
nurse had fallen through, and that the girl had
taken up with his best friend instead. The news
brought mixed feelings. It was up to him to contact
her again if he really cared.

There was a bulky package waiting for her at the
hall porter's office when she got back to Highcastle.
Her leave and her tenancy of the flatlet ended
officially two days later and she would have to
move her belongings out pretty quickly. She eyed
the parcel speculatively as she made her way
upstairs with her case. Her name was printed on it

and gave no clue to its source.

Inside was a fleecy-lined anorak of brilliant kingfisher blue. It was just the right size and eagerly she tried it on. It would keep her warm during her stay with Mrs Bland. Northern winters were generally much colder than London ones, with snow-drifts on occasions, and she had already shivered through one winter. Pleased though she was with the gift, she was perplexed. Surely it couldn't be for her? Yes, there was her name on the outside. Could it be David and Lynne Hanington? she wondered. Yet it was expensive, and they could not afford such a gift.

Surely not Paul—? Unbidden, memories of that day out with Adam came back—the walk through the fishing village, Adam lending her his jacket because the wind was chilling her. A cry broke from her and she buried her face in the anorak while she cried quietly. He didn't want her to catch cold. He *cared* about her!

'Oh, Adam! I love you!' she sobbed, half hoping the man himself would appear so she could thank him properly. The only way to do that was to offer him what he wanted—a loan of her love. She resolved that if the opportunity arose, she would offer him just that. If she could never be his wife she could, at least, enjoy his love for a brief while, and try to make him happy.

Two days later Isobel began her duties with Mrs Bland. Just before she set out on the journey she had the opportunity for which she had hoped—a chance to speak to Adam.

Joy Mackenzie was off duty and had come in

especially to help Isobel pack, and it was Joy who answered the door to Adam.

Isobel went white when she saw him, and Joy stepped back in surprise. Isobel knew the gossipy SEN couldn't wait to tell Sister Sowerby of this unexpected event.

Joy didn't have the tact to leave them alone, and Isobel wasn't sure if she was pleased or sorry. Adam stood in grim silence as the girls finished packing. He looked weary, the fine grey eyes dark and brooding, particularly when they rested upon Isobel. For her part, she longed to throw herself in his arms and confess her love, but she dared not. Even if they were alone she knew she didn't have the temerity to do such a thing.

The anorak was at the bottom of the smaller case and she made a pretence of repacking it, carefully folding the garment and replacing it. There was no response from Adam as he watched, and she began to doubt that he had sent it. Yet if not Adam Sheridan, then who?

She re-folded the anorak yet again, giving him another chance. He couldn't say anything in front of the other nurse, of course, but he could at least give her a clue, smile, or wink, surely? In the event, he didn't, and Isobel was left still wondering.

'For heaven's sake, Isobel!' exclaimed Joy, prising the anorak away from her. 'You've packed that at least a dozen times!'

She flushed, casting a sidelong glance at Adam, but he was gazing out of the window, lost in thought. Frustrated, she almost squashed the case when she sat on it to close it. It was over-full, but she wasn't going to unpack the anorak again! She began to wish she'd never seen the wretched garment.

At last Joy left when the consultant assured her that he would help Isobel downstairs with her luggage.

Left alone with him at last, Isobel didn't know what to say or how to say it. 'Thank you for helping me with my cases,' she said softly, her voice husky with the great effort she was making not to break down.

'My pleasure.' His tone was cool, professional, and her lips trembled.

'Oh, Adam!' she burst out, ready to fly into his arms if he gave her the slightest encouragement. But he did not. Grim-faced and silent, he picked up the two cases and walked out, leaving her to bring her transistor radio and a couple of bags crammed with odd bits and pieces.

He helped her into her small car with the cases, and she could bear the tense silence no longer. 'Adam, what is it? What have I done!' she cried.

'Did you enjoy your holiday?'

She stared blankly. 'Holiday? Yes, I suppose I did. It was only a few days, though. I went to London,' she added as he continued to stare moodily at her.

'I know.' His tone was clipped, and she sensed the leashed anger in him. Grey eyes bored into hers. 'Your lover telephoned and asked if you'd returned safely.'

'What lover?'

He frowned ominously. 'Don't you mean *which* lover?' he suggested, and her eyes blazed defiance at him.

'You're unspeakably insolent, Adam Sheridan! And arrogant, and selfish and . . . insufferable!' she added, managing at last to find a word that fitted him admirably.

'Do you deny you spent your holiday with Dr Ashe?' he demanded, and Isobel was about to deny it vehemently, then decided against it. Why bother? Clearly he wasn't going to believe her. He must have misunderstood something Paul said. Paul must have been asking whether she was still in London or had started her private nursing. The fact that Adam had immediately jumped to the obvious conclusion angered her, and filled her with a sorrow too deep for mere words.

With as much dignity as she could muster, she thanked him again for his help. Then, head held proudly, she got into her car and set off on the short journey to her new life. Nevertheless, she could not help glancing in the mirror as she drove off. Adam, hands in pockets, was still there, watching, as she turned out of the hospital car park.

She drove all the way with tears slowly coursing down her cheeks. He would never know how much his accusation had hurt her. Never again, she vowed, would she open her innermost heart to him, let him see how much she cared. She was finished with Adam Sheridan.

Mrs Bland was delighted to see her. So was her housekeeper/companion, Mrs Pullen. The housekeeper showed her to a spacious bedroom. It was on the ground floor, next to Mrs Bland's, and there was plenty of room for all her personal treasures. She would share Mrs Pullen's bathroom as Mrs Bland liked to keep her bathroom to herself.

'Got all her bits and bobs spread out how she likes,' Mrs Pullen explained. 'I'll show you her bathroom, though. Mrs Bland thought you'd be interested in the gadgets.'

The 'gadgets' were aids for the disabled, and it was clear the room had been specially adapted for the patient, as had the rest of the house. There was a lifting hoist for the nurse's use when Mrs Bland was unable to manage herself.

'She prefers to get into the big bath if she can,' the housekeeper explained. 'When she's poorly, she sits in this.' She indicated the medi-bath, a familiar piece of equipment to Isobel. Superficially it resembled a sitting-down shower unit. The patient sat on a seat while water was pumped in to whatever level she wished. She could then enjoy the luxury of a bath-cum-shower without the difficulty of getting in and out of a conventional low bath.

Afterwards Isobel had coffee with her patient and learned more about her abilities and disabilities. 'My doctor visits once a fortnight,' she explained. 'Now you're here that won't be necessary. How is dear Adam?' she went on, almost as an afterthought, and Isobel hesitated.

She licked her dry lips. 'He's well, I think. We've been so busy on the ward that I haven't seen much of him lately,' she hurried on.

'He *is* a busy man,' Mrs Bland agreed. 'Then there's all the work on the Home, and in addition he has to spend *some* time with his fiancée. Charming girl.'

Isobel agreed that Miss Kenlow was a charming girl, and fervently wished it to be true!

She carefully noted down all the relevant information about Mrs Bland's routine, medication and personal likes and dislikes. She no longer had a car, but friends often took her out for a drive. Isobel explained that her own car would be too small to allow ease of access for the woman, but Mrs Bland assured her she had enough outings as it was.

'Adam Sheridan often pops in and he takes me out whenever he can spare the time. Then there's Sonia. There's ample room in her car, but . . .' She paused, then went on slowly: 'I don't like to impose upon Sonia because I might become unwell and upset her.'

Isobel murmured an appropriate comment, thinking that Mrs Bland and the consultant spent too much time considering Sonia Kenlow's feelings. It was no business of hers, though, and she accepted that she might be just a teeny bit jealous of Adam's intended!

Two busy days passed, with Isobel settling down happily into her new routine. Mrs Pullen, a sixty-year-old widow, ran the home and did the shopping and cooking, so Isobel would have no household duties to perform except for keeping the patient's bedroom and bathroom tidy and making the bed.

Mrs Bland attended a private clinic for physiotherapy twice a week and found this beneficial. It was often morale-boosting but did not always, Isobel felt, bring any real benefit to the patient in the physical sense.

She did wonder, before she started working for Mrs Bland, why the woman needed a trained nurse.

Adam himself had explained that the disease was still in remission. Having spent two days there Isobel had her unspoken question answered. The period of remission appeared to be coming to an end but, even so, Mrs Bland still managed quite well. However, she needed supervising, needed someone to see that she didn't overtire herself, took her medication, rested whenever she was fatigued. Left to herself she did not, according to Mrs Pullen, keep to a routine. And if she didn't happen to agree with her GP and the neurologist, she would simply ignore their advice! She tended to make light of her symptoms, and Adam evidently thought it necessary for someone trained to report those symptoms to the doctors, for certainly Mrs Bland would not.

Mrs Bland had asked Adam to find a nurse for her, once he had bullied her into having one, and that was where Isobel came in.

When they arrived back from physiotherapy the following day they found Adam waiting for them. It was the first time she had seen him since his accusation about Paul being her lover, and she was deliberately cool, inventing an excuse to leave patient and doctor alone once she had settled Mrs Bland comfortably.

She was tidying Mrs Bland's locker when Adam appeared in the bedroom doorway. She felt his presence even before he spoke. 'How are you getting on, Bella?'

She turned, intent on giving him a brilliant but cold smile, but one look at his stricken face and she forgot her foolish notions.

Forgetting her pride too, she ran to his side,

putting her hand on his arm, her small fingers
kneading his jacket. 'What is it, Adam? Something's happened.'

'Mrs Chipchase died in the night. I thought you
would want to know.'

'Oh, no!' Her dear Mrs Chipchase, so brave in
adversity, so cheerful, too. 'I was going to see her
on my day off,' she said unhappily.

'It was only a matter of time. Some we win, some
we lose, Bella.' His voice was soft, friendlier now,
and she managed a wan smile.

'Why don't you have lunch with me on your
day off? I'm sure I could manage an hour or so.'
Grey eyes surveyed her dispassionately, and
she swallowed the lump in her throat. Grieving
for Mrs Chipchase would get her nowhere. Her
responsibilities were to Mrs Bland.

'I'd like that, but I'm not sure when I'm off duty.
Mrs Bland said I would have ample free time, but
. . .' There was nowhere in particular she wanted to
go on her off-duty.

'Are you missing him, Bella?' he demanded,
changing, like the chameleon, so swiftly that she
was nonplussed.

'If you mean Paul—no! There's no reason to miss
him. I—'

Mrs Pullen hovered in the doorway. 'Sorry to
disturb you when you're discussing medical matters,' she began affably, 'but there's a phone call for
you, Isobel. Your young man ringing all the way
from London!'

Adam Sheridan hissed—at least that was what it
sounded like to Isobel in her tense and jumpy state.
'That takes care of your days off, then, doesn't it!'

he snarled, and Isobel rounded on him angrily, once Mrs Pullen had gone.

'Listen to me, Adam Sheridan!' she began, necessarily having to keep her voice down. The sitting-room was only two doors away and there was nothing wrong with her employer's hearing. 'My private life is no business of yours!' she continued, then backed away from the fury in his eyes.

'It *is* my business if it interferes with your nursing duties, young woman,' he said grimly.

'Well, it won't!' she retorted, tears springing to her eyes. He was hateful! Sonia Kenlow was more than welcome to him! She hurried to the telephone in the hall, glad that Paul was ringing.

He was coming up just for an overnight stay in the middle of the following week, and Isobel arranged with Mrs Bland to have a day off then. It was agreed that she would have one day off during the week plus most weekends. That seemed over-generous, but when she protested Mrs Bland pointed out that she was on duty almost every evening and that she probably worked longer hours than she did in the hospital.

Adam seemed to approve the generous time off, but muttered something unintelligible when he heard that she was spending her day off with Paul Ashe.

Aware of Adam's scowling countenance, Isobel was extra sweet to Paul on the phone, once she had sorted out the days off with Mrs Bland.

'I hope you have a pleasant day,' Adam ground out once she had rung off.

'I'm sure I shall, Dr Sheridan,' she retorted, her flashing eyes daring him to retaliate.

A slow smile spread across his face. 'Round one to you, Nurse Ford.'

Isobel smiled back, ashamed of her outburst of temperament. 'We'll share the round, shall we?' she suggested impishly, and he laughed outright.

Mrs Bland came out of her sitting-room to find out the cause of the merriment, and Adam dropped a kiss on her brow. 'Just a medical joke, June,' he assured her, before dashing back to Highcastle General, where he had a clinic.

Isobel was touched that he had made the journey especially to tell her of Mrs Chipchase's death, and she explained about the woman. She thought it might not be very tactful to tell her of a patient who had died from the same disease, but gradually Mrs Bland got the information out of her.

'It's very sad, Isobel. Yet I know two other people with multiple sclerosis and they're both still enjoying a full life. It doesn't upset me to hear about the death, so don't worry,' she went on kindly. 'We must all die of something, and there *are* worse things than multiple sclerosis.'

Isobel was about to agree, when they had another visitor—Sonia Kenlow.

'There now!' Mrs Bland exclaimed, once Sonia had joined them in the sitting-room. 'You've just missed your better half! He's been gone this half-hour, I should think.'

Clearly displeased, Sonia nevertheless settled herself for what appeared to be a long visit. Isobel felt awkward. She and Mrs Bland had been in the middle of a conversation, yet she felt she ought to leave the room, let the two women exchange gossip. She was, after all, a hired nurse, not a friend, and she knew Mrs Pullen, a companion of many years, always left Mrs Bland alone with any guests.

'If you'll excuse me . . .' she began, getting up, but Mrs Bland wouldn't hear of her leaving.

'There's no need to go! Sonia is an old friend. I was at school with her mother,' she explained. 'I expect she'll tell us about the alterations.'

That remark tempted Isobel to remain, even though Sonia tried to exclude her from the ensuing conversation.

Adam would, Sonia informed them, be selling his own house. He and Sonia wouldn't live in Sonia's old home but would probably use the gardener's cottage in the grounds, once the house itself had been converted. 'Or else we'll live in Newcastle,' she went on. 'Adam loves my flat in Newcastle,' she added, with a special smile for Isobel. The smile did not reach the chilly blue eyes, but Isobel smiled back, anyway. She didn't want to be bad friends with Sonia, and if the ultra-elegant brunette could make Adam happy, she would try to be pleased for him.

Sonia didn't know how much alteration had been carried out, and didn't seem to care. She had already moved out. She shrugged when Mrs Bland asked how many patients would be accommodated. 'Oh, half a dozen, I should think,' she said airily, waving her left hand in Isobel's direction. Adam's ring glinted and flashed as the delicately-boned hand described some point to Mrs Bland.

It was a beautiful ring—a ruby set in a circle of tiny diamonds, and Adam must have just bought it. Swallowing her natural envy, Isobel made a point of admiring the ring as she had not seen it before, and Sonia slipped it off her thin finger and held it in the palm of her hand.

'Here, try it on, Nurse,' she offered sweetly, and with trembling hands Isobel took it from her.

She turned it this way and that, watching the jewels flash, but refused to try it on. 'It's unlucky to do that, Miss Kenlow. But thank you, anyway.' She handed it back with a warm smile, and a sulky-faced Sonia Kenlow slipped it on before resuming her conversation with her friend.

Isobel was proud that she had hidden her feelings so well, but when the two women gossiped on about people she didn't know, she was able to make her escape.

Oh, Adam! her heart cried. If only you knew how I'm suffering!

CHAPTER ELEVEN

SONIA KENLOW called again the following day. Isobel had just returned from a visit to Mrs Bland's doctor, who had asked Isobel to keep an eye on developments. Above all, he stressed, the patient wasn't to be burdened with any worries.

While worry could not, by itself, cause multiple sclerosis, there was no doubt that it was debilitating. Mrs Bland felt weak enough without any added worries.

She greeted Sonia Kenlow warmly, making a great effort for her patient's sake, though Mrs Bland was lying down.

'Mrs Bland is resting, Miss Kenlow. She thinks she took too much exercise this morning,' Isobel told her. The exercises were some she insisted on doing, even when she felt fatigued, and Isobel had to be extra firm with her. Once she felt weary she was to stop, and no arguments!

'Bother,' muttered Sonia. 'Oh well, I won't disturb her. You can fetch me a coffee while I'm here.' She moved away before Isobel could open her mouth, then turned. 'And some writing paper and envelopes.' She disappeared into Mrs Bland's private study before Isobel could comment.

Crossly she made the coffee and fetched some writing materials. It wasn't her job to fetch and carry, but there wasn't anything else for her to do while the patient slept. Mrs Bland did, in fact, tell her to take a few hours off.

Sonia Kenlow didn't thank her for the coffee. 'You didn't sugar it, did you?' Then: 'I don't have *cold* milk, Nurse. I prefer hot.' She pushed the small tray back towards Isobel, who made no move to take it.

Making coffee was one thing, being treated like a serf was quite another! 'I'm off duty, Miss Kenlow,' she began calmly. 'I made your coffee because there's no one else to do so. I am *not* a servant,' she added, to drive the point home.

Sonia's expression was amazed. 'Mrs Bland *pays* you, doesn't she? I imagine there's little enough nursing for you to do. She expects you to make yourself useful in the house!' she flared. 'I should like hot milk. Bring it now and no more will be said of your insolence.'

Before an angry Isobel could retort, another voice broke in: 'Isobel isn't a domestic, Sonia dear. She's a trained nurse.' June Bland, in satin dressing-gown, eased her tired body into the room, and Sonia went crimson.

Isobel, embarrassed, quickly picked up the tray with the offending coffee and hurried out to the kitchen. Her hands shook as she made fresh coffee and heated enough milk for the two women.

When she carried the tray back she found Mrs Bland alone. 'Sonia's gone. She had a hairdressing appointment.'

'I brought the hot milk she requested,' Isobel told her. 'Would you like coffee or just the milk?'

'Coffee, thank you. From what I heard she didn't *request* hot milk, she *demanded* it.' Mrs Bland eyed her shrewdly and Isobel wondered if she suspected that she loved Adam Sheridan just as much as Sonia Kenlow did. 'I can't understand what came over Sonia,' Mrs Bland added. 'She's such a charming girl.'

'Perhaps she isn't feeling well,' Isobel suggested, not wanting to say that Sonia was jealous of Adam's interest in her. The whole thing was ridiculous. Sonia wore his ring, was confident of his love. Why on earth should she resent a mere nurse?

That she *did* resent Isobel was evident the following day, because Adam paid an early morning visit to the house, before Mrs Bland was up. Isobel eyed him defiantly, sensing that he was in one of his moods. Even here she could not escape them!

'I thought you were spending the day with your . . . friend,' he began, eyes bleak.

Isobel raised a brow. 'I am, but first I have to help Mrs Bland get washed and dressed. Then I'm free the rest of the day.'

'Can't she manage? Are you trying to make yourself indispensable?'

She struggled with her temper. 'No one is indispensable, but she likes her clothes laid out for her. She can't brush her hair, either.'

'Why? Is the numbness returning?' he wanted to know.

Quickly she filled him in with the medical details.

'She hasn't had a nurse for about a year. It's as well you came,' he surprised her by saying.

A warm glow filled her heart, then he frowned at her. 'Sonia was in tears yesterday. Why did you have to be so unpleasant to her? She's a sensitive creature,' he added coldly.

Isobel was at a loss for words. All she could
splutter was: 'Sensitive? Her?' Then she closed her
mouth firmly. Hear no evil, see no evil, and speak
no evil, she admonished herself. She wasn't a person to carry tales, and no matter what she said he
would take Sonia's part.

'She's going to apologise next time she sees you,'
he went on, glaring at her.

'Apologise?' she echoed weakly.

'Yes!' he rasped. 'She offended you, apparently,
by asking you to make her a cup of coffee. She
didn't realise you would mind so much.'

Isobel closed her eyes, feeling as if her whole
world was spinning. Sonia Kenlow had Adam
exactly where she wanted him. Was he so blind
that he couldn't see what she was doing? 'Love is
blind,' she said clearly, leaving him to put what
interpretation he would on her remark.

'Yes, I suppose it is. You persist in this on-off
romance with a young man who quite obviously is
using you!' he flung at her.

'Paul? Is he?'

'As you say—love is blind. I won't disturb June.
Give her my love.' He strode out, leaving an angry
and helpless Isobel. They were farther apart than
ever. And Christmas came nearer every day.

The day out with Paul wasn't a success. To begin
with it started to rain, so Paul was reluctant to drive
far. Then he ran out of petrol in the wilds and had to
walk nearly two miles to the nearest garage. The
fact that Isobel walked with him did not sweeten his
temper to any marked degree, and he railed against
her for taking a job without self-contained accommodation. 'You could at least have demanded a

sitting-room!' he grumbled, as they reached the service station at last.

'So we could have a cosy day on the settee?' she suggested bitterly.

'Why not? I *have* come a long way.' His voice was plaintive, but Isobel didn't feel in a forgiving mood.

Although she didn't nag him or make any reference to her ruined day off, they were barely speaking by the time Paul took her back to Mrs Bland's. The sight of Adam's car in front of the house did nothing to improve her temper. She supposed he was going to tell her off again. Perhaps his fiancée had suffered a nervous breakdown and, of course, Nurse Isobel Ford would be to blame!

Adam strolled out of the house just as Paul gathered her in his arms. She began to struggle, then, seeing Adam watching, she pretended instead that she was enjoying Paul's kisses. She didn't want Adam to know how unhappy she was.

'I hope your chief's enjoying the view!' Paul chuckled as he nuzzled her neck.

Isobel squirmed, managing to free herself without the struggle being obvious to the watching consultant. 'Thank you for a lovely day, Paul,' she said untruthfully, and he flashed her a brilliant smile, no doubt convinced that it *had* been a lovely day apart from the two-mile walk!

Once she was out of the car she imagined he would drive off, but he followed her as she walked slowly towards the front door and Adam Sheridan.

'I thought you ought to be the first to know, sir,' Paul began, beaming at Adam. 'Isobel has finally agreed to marry me!'

Thunderstruck, Isobel could do no more than

stand helplessly as Adam gravely congratulated them both. She started to speak, then saw the consultant's fiancée just coming out of the house. Instead, she laughed like a girl in love and thanked Adam politely for his good wishes.

Of course Sonia had to be introduced to the charismatic Paul Ashe, and it was clear that she found him charming—so much so that she invited them to dine with her when Paul was next in Northumberland!

Swallowing her pride, Isobel apologised briefly for the coffee episode the previous day—an apology which was reciprocated by Sonia Kenlow. Adam stood watching them, eyes hooded. Whatever he thought of the episode, he was keeping his own counsel.

Mrs Bland was spending the weekend with friends in Hexham, and Isobel wondered whether she ought to go with her. It didn't matter if she couldn't have the weekend off. Paul had returned to London after promising to telephone her the next evening. She could ring Joy Mackenzie, she supposed, or David's wife, but she would be content to spend the weekend quietly if Mrs Bland didn't need her.

'No, no, Isobel, you have your weekend off,' Mrs Bland insisted, when Isobel tentatively offered to accompany her. 'My friend is a trained nurse and she'll see me all right. You enjoy the weekend. Have some friends in if you like,' she suggested.

Isobel was touched by the kind offer. Mrs Bland always did her best to make her feel at home, and was careful never to imply that she was a paid servant, but it was awkward at times. As Adam said, it took a special person to nurse someone like Mrs Bland in her own home, and Isobel wasn't sure she fitted that description. Being a private nurse was a bit like being a nanny, she supposed. One was neither a servant nor a member of the family; it was a kind of no-man's-land.

It wasn't as rewarding as hospital nursing, either, she reflected, on the Saturday morning after she had waved Mrs Bland off. The money was good and Isobel felt her patient was over-generous since free meals were provided as well, but the post lacked job-satisfaction and Isobel didn't know how long she would continue there. It all depended upon Mrs Bland's condition. Although she liked help in the mornings with dressing she didn't actually need a *trained* nurse. An auxiliary would do just as well, though evidently Adam Sheridan didn't think so. Though there remained the question of the signs and symptoms Mrs Bland kept to herself.

It was hot, with a brilliant sun beating down, and a lazy morning on the sun-bed appealed to her. Quickly she finished her few chores, leaving the house tidy, then changed out of her uniform into a cerise and white striped bikini. The uniform dress was similar to those she had worn in London, a simply-designed white checked dress, which was pleasantly cool. No starched collar and cuffs! With it she wore her navy belt and silver SRN's buckle but no cap. That was just as well; at Highcastle she could never keep her cap on her unruly hair.

She took the pins out of her hair and ran a brush through it. It crackled and glowed with health and vitality, though it needed cutting, she decided,

thinking she might ask Mrs Pullen. The housekeeper was away for the day but would be back
tonight, and Isobel intended having a meal ready
for her as a surprise. Busy with thoughts of
menus, she didn't see Adam until she bumped into
him.

'Oh! It's you!' she exclaimed. 'Mrs Bland is away
for the weekend!'

'Is she? That's very remiss of her,' he said mildly.
His dark gaze swept over her bikini-clad form and
she wished the garment wasn't so brief. She felt
naked, though that was ridiculous. He wouldn't get
over-excited by the female form; he saw enough
partially clothed bodies in the course of his work.
But not *my* body; her brain protested. He hasn't
seen *me* so scantily dressed!

She could feel the warm tide of colour sweep
over her face, and the blush must have been noticeable, for Adam gave his husky chuckle—a sensuous, exciting sound that caused her to blush the
more. 'I'm just going to sunbathe,' she said at last,
brushing past him and making for the dubious
sanctuary of the sun-bed.

To her great relief he didn't follow her, and her
overheated face and body gradually cooled down.
She wished she'd brought a wrap or a towel, but she
was unwilling to venture into the house while he
was there. He was probably writing a note for Mrs
Bland and would be only a few minutes.

She put on her sunglasses, then reached for the
bottle of sun-oil. Being so fair-skinned and freckled
she wasn't a sun-worshipper. Ten minutes or so
would be enough sunbathing, then she would move
into the shade. Just ten minutes, letting the heat of

the sun lull her into believing she was on some tropical isle, alone except for Adam Sheridan.

Smiling to herself, she opened the bottle. Then suddenly it was plucked from her hands and her startled gaze met that of the consultant.

He, too, had come prepared for a relaxing day in the garden. In jeans and casual checked shirt he looked years younger, less careworn, particularly when he smiled down at her.

Isobel smiled back, unable to conceal her pleasure at sight of him. Although he belonged to Sonia Kenlow, she couldn't help loving him. What did one stolen hour matter? she mused drowsily, as he gently rubbed the oil into her warm skin.

Obediently she sat up while he attended to her back, moving the bra straps aside. It was a curiously sexless gesture, and her heart swelled with love for him. Paul would have deftly removed the bra, she knew from bitter experience of last summer. She shivered at the memory, haunted by those fears of frigidity with which Paul had taunted her.

Adam stopped immediately he felt her tremble and she wanted to scream at him: 'Don't worry! It isn't you—it's just a bad memory.'

'There—all done.' His voice was soft, soothing, and she lay down again and closed her eyes after murmuring her thanks. Adam Sheridan was conscious of his own masculinity, his own identity; he did not need to prove a point by making love to her. With him she was safe. So she slept, knowing that he would awaken her when it was time to lie in the shade. This was true love.

She was only half-awake when he moved her out of the sun. He carried her to the shade of one of the many trees, then brought over the sun-bed, scooping her up in his arms to deposit her gently on the bed. His arms stayed around her longer than was strictly necessary, and drowsily she reached up for him.

His kiss was feather-light, and she moaned, opening her eyes to gaze at his much-loved face. His expression was inscrutable, the eyes giving no indication of his feelings, and she was embarrassed at her own temerity. She must leave him to make the next move. Whatever he wanted she knew she would not deny him. It was wicked of her to steal from Sonia Kenlow, yet it would be only a brief while. He would still marry Sonia, there was no doubt of that.

Adam must have read the love in her eyes, for a groan broke from him. To Isobel, it sounded as if his very heart was groaning.

'Bella!' His voice was despairing, and she knew what happened next, if anything, was up to her. Her love gave her power over him and the emotion was heady. So much power to hold in her small hands, so much love she could give him if she chose.

Yet it was Adam who took control, contenting himself with kissing her soft, sun-warmed mouth. 'I'll get another sun-bed and join you. Don't go away, Bella!' Then he was gone, his long strides taking him to the garage where the garden furniture was kept.

With a half-sob Isobel sat up, hugging her knees to her chest. Of course she was proud of Adam, glad that he was not being unfaithful to his fiancée, yet . . . Yet she couldn't help wishing he *would* be unfaithful—with *her*!

When he returned he discarded his shirt, then stretched out beside her, pillowing his head upon his arms.

She shot him a quick glance out of the corner of her eye, her heartbeat racing at sight of his bare bronzed chest, the rippling muscles as he moved. As if aware of her scrutiny he turned to face her, his sun-bed squeaking in protest as he settled his heavy body more comfortably. They exchanged smiles, then, greatly daring, Isobel reached out and touched his hand. His fingers curled over hers.

In his eyes she read the declaration of love that his lips would not speak, and she was satisfied. He was faithful to Sonia, no matter how much he was tempted to be otherwise.

Hunger eventually drove them to a picnic lunch on the lawn, Isobel slipping a towelling robe over her bikini so as not to tempt Adam beyond endurance.

'Not cold enough for your anorak, then?' he commented, a gleam in his eye, and she laughed.

'It *was* you! I couldn't imagine who else might have sent it!'

'Ashe, maybe?' His tone was dry, the humour fading from his face, and she flushed, shaking her head decisively.

'No! Only you cared . . .' she hesitated, fearing to embarrass him, 'that I might get a cold without a warm jacket,' she finished lamely. 'Why didn't you tell me?' she rushed on. 'I kept repacking the darn thing right in front of your eyes!'

His smile was strained. 'I was angry with you for spending your holiday with Ashe. Stupid of me.' The cold eyes searched her face and must have read the truth there, for he smiled broadly this time, the grey eyes warming her.

Later, they sat companionably in the sun once it had lost its fiery heat, just talking. Isobel found that Adam shared her love of theatregoing and of Shakespeare in particular, though he confessed that he was a little surprised that she should like Shakespeare.

'It isn't just old fuddy-duddies who enjoy Shakespeare's plays!' she protested mildly. 'Our English teacher at school was a former actress and I think she regretted leaving the theatre. Some of her love of literature and great playwriting must have rubbed off on to me,' she said reflectively. 'I once played Feste in our end-of-term production of *Twelfth Night*!' she admitted, and Adam chuckled.

She watched him, her eyes dark with sadness despite the amusing memories. Evening would come too soon.

When he suggested they might one night make up a party to visit the theatre in Newcastle, she was delighted. Then her face fell as she realised that such a party would have to include Sonia and probably Paul as well.

'Paul!' she blurted out, as they packed up their picnic things. 'I'm not engaged to him!' Her eyes willed Adam to understand.

'I'm glad,' he said simply. 'I thought you had too much intelligence to marry an idiot like that, but when he said you were engaged, I began to wonder!' he admitted.

'I've told him that there's no point in coming up here again,' she added, letting him know that she, at least, was free. 'His girl-friend in London ran off with his best friend. That's why he's been pursuing me,' she finished flatly, hurt that she'd been so ill-used.

'I'm sure that isn't true, Bella. A handsome young chap like him probably has girls falling over themselves to beg for a date! He must have loved *you*, or wanted you, at any rate. Don't denigrate yourself.' He wagged an admonishing finger at her and she chuckled, her hurt pride salved by his comments. Perhaps Paul *did* love her, in his own way. As Adam said, there were lots of pretty nurses in London; he didn't need to make the long journey north just to find a girl.

When Paul telephoned and she had told him she couldn't marry him he had sounded thunderstruck. Yet she had been unyielding, pointing out that she was fond of him but wasn't yet ready to settle down. She didn't throw his words back at him about her being frigid, but no doubt that thought was in his mind when he finally accepted that she would not become his wife.

'I really love you, Isobel—honestly I do.' She could almost hear his plaintive tones and her eyes darkened. In his own way perhaps he did. And to think for nearly a year she'd been suffering a broken heart because she thought he *didn't* love her! All those months wasted, she reflected, but without bitterness. All that time I've been reaching for a dream, when the true love of my life has been right here in Northumberland.

When Adam learned that Mrs Pullen was due back that evening he said he would stay the night. 'I've got a busy week ahead of me and I could do with a weekend in the country,' he smiled.

Isobel wondered why he couldn't spend the weekend in his own charming country house, but of course she didn't comment on his decision—she was too delighted at the prospect of having him to herself all weekend!

He didn't mention Sonia Kenlow, nor did she. The woman cast a black shadow over them, nonetheless, and when the telephone shrilled later that evening Isobel was convinced it was Sonia, demanding to know if Adam was there. It wasn't, though; it was Mrs Pullen ringing to let Isobel know she was spending the night with her friend. She was apologetic, knowing that Isobel would be all alone in the big house, but Isobel reassured her by saying she had got friends in and they would be staying the night.

Adam overheard the conversation and he smiled wryly as she replaced the receiver. 'It looks as if we'll be alone, Bella. I can hardly leave now—I don't like to think of you alone out here.'

Isobel protested, mildly, that she would be perfectly secure. 'If I bolt the doors when you go, no one will be able to get in.' She hoped that he would insist on staying, though, and so it proved.

'I can't leave, but I can't stay,' he muttered, rubbing his chin reflectively. He needed another shave and that fact must have registered, for he slipped his jacket on, made sure that all the windows were closed and told Isobel she was to lock the door after him, that he wouldn't be long.

She did as she was bid, reflecting that in the country doors were not often locked.

He was soon back, bringing his toilet items and a

change of clothing. Her eyes widened when she saw the sleeping bag he carried into the study.

'Can't you have a bed?' she queried. 'There's a spare bedroom upstairs.'

'I know, but I don't want to make extra work for Mrs Pullen. I shall be comfortable enough,' he assured her, his smile strained.

How could she cope with sharing the same house? They would be together all night in an otherwise empty house, and desire had already sprung between them. It wouldn't take much more for them to spend the night in each other's arms.

The atmosphere became more strained as the evening wore on. Isobel switched on the huge colour TV in the sitting-room but was unable to concentrate on the programme. She watched the adverts during the commercial break as well—anything to keep her mind from the close proximity of the doctor who lounged in an armchair nearby.

She switched the TV off about eleven and glanced shyly over at Adam. His eyes were closed, his body relaxed, his breathing even, and waves of love stole over her. In sleep he was a far cry from the arrogant, quick-tempered consultant. He might have been her husband, dozing in his chair after a hard day's work.

Tears sprang to her eyes and she was thankful that he couldn't see them. Tenderly she draped one of Mrs Bland's tartan rugs across him, then crept from the room. She decided against turning out the light, fearing it would waken him.

'Sleep well, my darling.' Her lips silently formed the words as she closed her bedroom door and undressed. She had no fear of spending the night with Adam Sheridan, with only an unlocked door between them. He would never harm her; only if she encouraged him would there be danger. Even then, he seemed so totally in command of his feelings that he rarely lost control. One of the charms of the older man, she mused, then she drifted off to a dreamless and sound sleep.

All was quiet when she awoke next morning. Still only half awake, she slipped into her dressing-gown, then crept into the kitchen, intent on wakening Adam with a cup of coffee. But he had beaten her to it. A cup and saucer were left to drain and there were the remains of a loaf of bread on the table.

Isobel hurried through to the sitting-room where she had left him, but he wasn't there. She had seen him carry his sleeping-bag into the study, and the study door was closed. But when she opened the door the room was as empty and as neat and tidy as ever. The sleeping-bag was gone, too.

She sat at the kitchen table for ages, just thinking, dreaming of what might have been. The whole day stretched interminably ahead, empty and silent like the house. Her body longed for Adam's touch, her soul longed to hear his voice, his husky chuckle.

She knew he was right to leave, once daylight came. It was the correct thing for him to do, and she loved him all the more because he had behaved so correctly. That fact did nothing to ease her heartache, though!

Mrs Bland returned from her weekend looking fit and well. The dragging of her left foot had stopped as suddenly as it had started and she had had no more of the painful grimacing.

Isobel, by contrast, was anything but rested and it was hard to believe she had had the weekend to herself, with nothing to do except laze in the sun. Mrs Pullen had arrived back Sunday evening and even she had commented on Isobel's drawn expression, her pain-filled eyes.

Adam called the next evening with details of their proposed visit to the theatre. Isobel had almost forgotten, but when she found that Mrs Bland was looking forward to the trip, she forced enthusiasm into her voice and the three of them made plans, and several tentative dates were put forward.

'Sonia wanted to invite your friend Ashe, but I told her he would be too busy,' Adam put in, as Isobel at last met his intense gaze.

'I don't want him to come!' she said vehemently, and Mrs Bland gave her a strange look.

'Good. It will just be June, Sonia and yourself, then,' he said with satisfaction. He closed his diary with a snap, then asked to use Mrs Bland's telephone to make the bookings.

After Adam had made the arrangements he waylaid Isobel as she was about to make her escape into the garden. 'Just a minute, Bella,' he commanded. 'We have to talk.'

She spun round, tense and wary. Whatever he said would only turn the knife in the wound. Yet she would listen, if only for the pleasure of hearing his deep voice.

'I'm sorry I had to leave so precipitately on Sunday morning.' His voice was clipped, the dry tones of the professional physician, and Isobel forced a smile to her lips.

'I understood, Adam,' she assured him, seeking to put him at his ease. 'It . . . it was the best thing to do,' she added, trying to persuade herself that it was so.

'I'm sick and tired of doing what's best!' he exploded, to her great astonishment. 'What's best for everyone else isn't necessarily best for me!'

Before she could comment, he swept her into his arms, uncaring that they might be seen from the windows. His kiss was savage, masterful, almost despairing in its intensity.

Her lips tingled from contact with his mouth as he released her as abruptly as he had taken her in his arms. She put a hand to her burning mouth as he hurried to his car.

Her heart cried his name, her lips forming the words, 'I love you,' but he did not hear.

CHAPTER TWELVE

MRS BLAND enjoyed their visit to the theatre, but it was spoiled for Isobel. The play was one she hadn't seen before and within moments of the opening lines she was lost in it. Sonia's stage whispers soon put paid to that. She demanded to know what the play was about, whether Adam had seen it before, if Mrs Bland was comfortable and whether she would like a chocolate.

Admittedly, she was careful not to disturb the other patrons, but she took a special delight in disturbing Isobel, who longed to shake her. Later, over dinner, Sonia returned to the subject with which she had started their journey—the non-appearance of Paul Ashe.

'But he's your fiancé, Nurse! Surely he could get away?'

Adam came to Isobel's rescue as she was racking her brains for some suitable excuse. 'He's a busy man, Sonia. Junior doctors work long hours and he seems to have had a fair amont of off-duty. He must owe them some hours?' This last remark was addressed to Isobel, who was quick to agree.

'One of his friends has been covering for him and he has to work for the friend now,' she explained.

Sonia seemed dissatisfied with the explanation, until Adam pointed out mildly that when *she* was working she could never get away.

'That's different, darling!' she cooed. 'I work

when it pleases me! If I really wanted a day off when there's work in, I would take one.'

'That hasn't been my experience,' Adam commented. 'Work for Carl takes priority over anything *I* might want.'

'Oh, Adam! I do believe you're jealous!' Sonia's tinkling laugh rang out.

That conversation was interesting, Isobel mused, as she toyed with her meal. Adam had once told her that a wife's first duty was to be a helpmeet to her husband and that too many women tried to emulate big-business men. He must have been thinking of Sonia when he said that, and Isobel was curious to know who Carl was, and what kind of work Sonia did. Whatever the nature of her work, it could only be part-time, and she gave the impression of having plenty of leisure. Being a direct sort of girl she asked Sonia outright what she did for a living.

Sonia shot her a perplexed look as though wondering why she should be interested, yet she answered readily enough. Her enthusiasm for her work came across strongly, and Isobel wondered how poor Adam felt about it. Carl, it transpired, was an interior decorating consultant, and Sonia, who was artistic, did some of his designing.

'My designs for a Country Diary kitchen were praised by one of our foremost experts!' she boasted.

Clearly it was work she loved, though whether she also loved Carl wasn't clear. Throughout the catalogue of Sonia's achievements Adam sat silently, attentive to Mrs Bland's needs but otherwise in a world of his own, and Isobel felt for him. What Sonia did sounded interesting, exciting even, but it was a far cry from the medical world of Adam Sheridan and herself.

The attraction of opposites, she supposed, as they drove back. It had been agreed that Sonia would spend the night with Mrs Bland, Adam going on to his own house as he had to make an early start the following morning. He stayed at Mrs Bland's for coffee, though, and for a rest before driving home. It was then that he mentioned a patient with a blood disorder who had been admitted to Bladen just after Isobel left.

'She's got a kind of haemophilia,' he explained. 'It's very rare and isn't generally mentioned in textbooks. I've never come across a case before,' he went on, warming to his subject. Isobel leaned towards him, two minds intent on human problem-solving.

'Adam!' scolded Sonia, stalking over to perch on the arm of his chair. 'No talking shop! You can do that to your heart's content tomorrow when you're with your own people.'

'Nurse Ford *is* one of my own people,' he reminded Sonia, who reddened. 'She's a nurse, and I expect she misses her patients at Highcastle.'

'I'm sure they miss her,' Mrs Bland smiled.

'I know *I* do,' he affirmed, and it was Isobel's turn to flush, but with pleasure. Adam Sheridan actually missed her on the ward!

It was well after midnight when Sonia saw Adam off the premises. Isobel had helped settle Mrs Bland in bed a little before and was waiting to lock up once Sonia was back in the house. She tried not to let her imagination run riot, but it didn't take a lot of imagination to picture them kissing passionately once they were alone. To blot out the disquieting thought she busied herself in the kitchen.

When Sonia returned she carelessly slammed the front door and Isobel winced, fearful lest the sound irritate Mrs Bland. She was tempted to ask Sonia to be more careful about noise, but she knew it wasn't her place to do so. Whatever she said would be taken down, twisted and used in evidence against her! The coffee episode proved that.

Sonia and Adam must have quarrelled, for the woman's eyes were unnaturally bright. Isobel hesitated about saying anything, half wondering if she should invite Sonia to have a good cry. Then Sonia turned on her spitefully and she was glad she hadn't offered the olive branch.

'Adam says you've broken off your engagement,' Sonia began as soon as she had closed the kitchen door.

'Did he?' Isobel kept her voice even, non-committal. 'I shouldn't have thought it was any of his business.' She dried the last coffee cup and set it out on the table for breakfast, avoiding Sonia's gaze as she did so.

'He must have have thought it was his business!' Sonia snapped, as she began pacing up and down the long narrow kitchen. 'Why did you throw him over? Isn't a registrar good enough for you? You won't get Adam, you know!'

'I don't want Adam,' Isobel said slowly and distinctly. 'Now—*will you leave me alone!*' she snapped, driven beyond all endurance.

Sonia wasn't to be quelled. Although visibly taken aback by Isobel's unexpectedly spirited defence, she meant to have her say. 'I know you love Adam,' she began again, and Isobel sighed.

'I refuse to listen to you, Miss Kenlow,' she said firmly, making for the door, but the much taller woman moved swiftly to head off her retreat.

'Just you listen to me, Little Miss Nurse!' Seeing that there was no escape, Isobel perched on the corner of the big kitchen table and crossly folded her arms. She was desperately tired and hoped Sonia would not take long to propound her theories. 'I know Adam doesn't love me,' Sonia went on more calmly, as she leant against the door. Her brooding blue eyes were fixed upon Isobel, who felt uncomfortable under their scrutiny.

She felt even more uncomfortable a moment later when she was told she must leave Mrs Bland's employ.

'Leave!' she squeaked. 'Why should I? If Adam doesn't love you, my leaving won't make any difference.'

Sonia shrugged. 'You could be right,' she agreed. 'But I don't want you around and that's final! You love him. He must have seen the lovesick calf looks you keep giving him!' she cried.

Isobel didn't care to be likened to a lovesick calf, but because she could not deny the accusation of loving Adam Sheridan, she kept silent. Apparently taking this as evidence of guilt, Sonia went on to dictate her terms. 'Adam is interested only in my home, in turning it into a refuge for his wretched patients. If you leave he can still go ahead with his plans. If not—' She paused significantly and Isobel began to protest, aware that protest was futile and that Sonia Kenlow held all the cards.

'I love him and I happen to believe that I will make an excellent consultant's wife,' Sonia went on, cutting short Isobel's protests. 'A rich wife is always a help,' she added, and Isobel silently agreed. 'I'm prepared to marry him,' she went on, morosely surveying her engagement ring, 'even knowing that he doesn't love me. He wants my home, and unless you leave and move right away, he won't get it.'

Isobel, furious, was about to tell Sonia what she could do with her orders, but seeing the anger in her face, Sonia decided on a quick retreat. Isobel was left half sobbing with frustration and anger. How could that woman treat Adam like that? How could Adam be so blind? Surely he must realise how tenacious Sonia Kenlow was, how determined?

She lay sleepless on top of her bed for what remained of the night, turning Sonia's threat over and over in her mind. She could not believe that the other woman would be so vicious. Yet clearly she was jealous of Isobel, and jealousy was a powerful motive for many crimes. Taking away Adam's chance of a Home for his disabled patients *was* a crime, of that Isobel was in no doubt.

Eventually she dozed off, and slept late because she had forgotten to set her alarm. It was nearly ten when the sunlight streaming through her window at last woke her. Another crime to lay at Miss Kenlow's door! Being late on duty was something Isobel abhorred. Poor Mrs Bland liked help in the bathroom.

Her patient brushed aside Isobel's apologies with a smile. 'It's nonsense for you to feel guilty, my dear. I managed perfectly well. I do believe I'm getting better!' Proudly she showed how well she was walking now, and announced that it must be the physio which was helping her.

'I'm glad,' Isobel said cautiously. 'Is your vision better, too? I told Dr Greene that your left eye was bothering you again.'

The woman hesitated, apparently unwilling to admit to fresh disabilities. 'The blurring comes and goes. But I'm fine at the moment,' she assured Isobel blithely.

She must see Adam, Isobel decided—explain all this to him and await his instructions. Although Mrs Bland had a private doctor and was under the care of the local neurologist, she seemed to take more notice of Adam's opinion.

It was suprising how much they relied on Adam, she reflected later that day when she had a few hours to herself. She had come to think of him as the fount of all wisdom, just as her patient did. It was comforting to know that he wasn't far away, that he cared deeply.

She had decided to ignore Sonia's threat, believing it to be an empty one. If work had already started on converting her home it was unlikely she would wish, or be able, to stop it now. If she did so, Adam would finish with her, Isobel was certain of that. As long as she herself kept away from Adam, except for professional purposes, all would be well. Any personal happiness for which she hoped must be sacrificed to a good cause.

Theory is easier than practice, and it wasn't easy to keep out of the consultant's way. Because she wanted to mention the blurred vision without Mrs

Bland knowing, she decided to drive to the hospital, hoping for a few minutes' conversation with him. She was out of luck as he had a crowded clinic, and wouldn't be finished until it was time for her to return to her duties. She left a message with his secretary, then took a detour on the way back, taking in Sonia Kenlow's house.

There was no sign of life, and Isobel was puzzled that the workmen's transport was missing. Then realisation came. Sonia Kenlow had acted already. Work had been stopped on Adam's project!

Knowing that she was the cause of this calamity made her feel quite sick, and she sat in her car for several minutes, fighting down nausea and an impotent rage. For there was nothing she could do. Nothing at all. Except leave Mrs Bland and never set eyes on Adam again, a little voice reminded her. You know Sonia Kenlow's terms. Act upon them. Leave *now*, before the damage is irreversible.

Yet she could not. Mrs Bland still needed a vigilant eye kept on her, even if she didn't think so.

In answer to her message, Adam telephoned that evening, apologising briefly for being unable to get away. 'I've got some notes to write up, then we're off to a consultants' dinner,' he explained.

Isobel assured him she understood, all the while wondering whether he knew that work had stopped on the Home. If he knew it was odd that he didn't mention it. He seemed out of humour, but that was Adam Sheridan! Moody as they came, but never with the patients. Longing swept over her as they talked. Even though he often took his bad humour out on her, she did so want to be back at

Highcastle Hospital, working with him, moods and all.

She explained briefly about her patient, and he promised to have to look at her the following day, Saturday. 'Is there anything else?' he added. There was her opportunity to mention the house, yet she was afraid to.

'No, there's nothing else,' she said flatly, replacing the receiver. When Adam found out that work had stopped, he would naturally blame her. She must try to put matters right before that happened.

Dr Greene, when she called to see him that evening, assured her that Mrs Bland was doing well. Fussing over her, he pointed out, would only make her angry. And the anger would debilitate her and make the symptoms worse. An argument might well bring on the neuralgia, though this could happen at any time.

Satisfied with her patient's progress yet fearing to make her angry, Isobel quietly told her she wanted to leave.

The woman looked blank. 'Leave? You haven't been here five minutes!' she protested, and Isobel flushed.

'That's true, but . . .' she began, only to be waved down.

'I should miss you, Isobel. You can't possibly leave, because I won't accept your resignation. I'm sure Adam will be astonished,' she went on, her glance sharp.

Isobel coloured all the more, and Mrs Bland nodded to herself as if she'd proved a point.

No more was said on the subject that evening, and sleeping on the problem produced no ready solution for Isobel. She must leave. Yet she hesitated to upset her patient. What Adam would say did not bear thinking about!

Predictably, he was furious. Angry grey eyes snapped at her as she tried to explain the next morning. Since she had no particular reason for wanting to leave it made it more awkward. She had thought out what she would say to him, but once she was confronted by the anger of the man she loved, her carefully prepared story never got off the ground.

'If you leave now, I'll never forgive you, Bella!' he stormed. 'You're letting yourself down, as well as June Bland.' He paused, eyes narrowed suspiciously, and Isobel wondered what was coming next. 'Has leaving got anything to do with Ashe?' he demanded.

She opened her mouth to deny the charge, then reconsidered. Why not let him believe she was going to marry Paul, after all? That was an excellent excuse for leaving, one that the patient would accept as well. 'I've missed him, if that's what you mean,' she admitted. 'I've missed London, too. The prospect of another winter up here isn't all that inviting,' she added for good measure.

Adam's face was like thunder and she thought he was about to shake her. Instead, he made a helpless gesture. 'All right, go to him, if that's what you want. Go to the devil for all I care!'

'You're the devil, and I'm certainly not coming to *you*!' she flung at him. 'Why should I always be a punchbag for your . . . your verbal violence!' she stormed. 'You hate me because I'm young, because I'm a southerner, because . . .' She couldn't think of any other reasons, but surely she'd given him enough?

'Do I, Bella? I didn't know.' His voice was weary and she fought down the desire to throw herself into his arms and comfort him, tell him she didn't mean all the nasty things she'd said.

They eyed each other warily after their storm, and Isobel waited for him to speak first. An odd smile curved the corners of his stern mouth. 'I shall miss you, Bella. Think it over carefully before you burn your boats.'

She met his gaze steadfastly. 'I *have* thought it over, Adam. Believe me, it's for the best.' How much for the best he would never know.

'Let's part amicably, then.' He held out his hand in a gesture of reconciliation, and she forced herself to place her hand in his, praying that the tears would hold off until she was alone.

He drew her towards him, and she tried to still her trembling body but could not. Every nerve jangled as he kissed her gently on the brow. Then he left, her green eyes following his tall figure until he reached his car.

It was all over. Isobel had fulfilled her part of the bargain. What happened next was up to Sonia Kenlow.

Agency nursing did not really suit Isobel's temperament; she preferred the more structured nursing possible in a ward and missed the company of other nurses. Of course, she had a wide variety of patients, many of them cancer sufferers.

After much thought she had elected to do night nursing. She could always change back to days some time in the future. Or she might seek a post in a Northumberland hospital some considerable way from Highcastle and Adam Sheridan! For the moment, though, she would keep away from the local hospitals.

Seeing that Isobel was determined to leave, Mrs Bland put no further obstacles in the way of her leaving. However, she insisted on hearing the truth, and that placed Isobel in a quandary. Sonia Kenlow and Mrs Bland were friends; there was no way she could blacken the other woman's character. Even if Mrs Bland believed the accusation, telling her would do more harm than good. In a fit of spite Sonia would see that her home never became the refuge for patients for which Adam was hoping.

In the end she told part of the truth: that she had finished completely with Paul and would make no attempt to see him again. She pointed out, also truthfully, that Mrs Bland didn't actually need a trained nurse at present.

Her patient had acknowledged the fact quietly, then asked Isobel, point-blank, if she was in love with Adam Sheridan. Her face must have given Mrs Bland the answer to *that* question, and no more was said on the matter.

Now it was morning and another night's work was over. Her patient, an elderly man, was dying. For him, soon, morning would never come, yet to the old and suffering death came as a friend, and she tried not to be too sad for him. She stroked his hand tenderly before she left. Now she was on nights off and didn't know if she would be sent back to him when she returned to duty.

As Sister Sowerby had once said, even for the terminal patient there was always something positive a nurse could do, even if it was only to share a few snippets of gossip or wipe away a tear. Sad that her knowledge could not cure all the sick people on her list, she walked with bowed head to her small car and drove off.

She liked to drive out into the country after duty before going back to her lodgings to sleep. Of course, with leaving Mrs Bland she had also to leave her accommodation, and finding a flat was proving to be difficult. At the moment she had inexpensive and relatively quiet lodgings in Newcastle itself, and now she turned the car in that direction, feeling the urge to wash and change before spending the day by the sea. She could doze in the car, perhaps. It was a beautiful day and there seemed little sense in going to bed when she could sleep tonight.

Some of her belongings were still at Mrs Bland's and there was no hurry to collect them, she had been assured. Still . . . better to sever *all* ties as soon as possible, she decided, resting in her room until it was a more civilised hour for visiting. If she left it until mid-morning Sonia might well be there, and she could do without another confrontation.

It was only two weeks since she had left, yet it seemed as if she'd been away years. Mrs Bland and the housekeeper hugged and kissed her, and she was pleased to see how well her former patient looked. Adam had found her a part-time SEN, who lived locally, and Isobel thought that was better for her. She could manage most of the time and didn't really like to be chivvied about.

Isobel collected her bits and pieces and stowed them in the car, keeping a happy smile pinned to her mouth all the while. Nothing of her agony must show or Mrs Bland would be quick to report it to Adam. She didn't ask after Adam, Sonia or the Home, and Mrs Bland volunteered no information.

After eliciting the information that Isobel was heading for a secluded spot on the coast, Mrs Bland waved goodbye.

Indeed, she was halfway to the coast before she decided she couldn't face it after all. There probably wouldn't be any crowds, but one never knew. She had intended to visit the little fishing hamlet to which Adam had once taken her, but she couldn't remember its name. That was the only place she wanted to visit, and she almost cried when she realised she could not. She was too tired to drive around in search of it and she resolved to do so the next day.

Instead, she found herself on the road to Hadrian's Wall, or part of it, for it was very long, some seventy miles or more. She left the car in a small car-park provided for tourists visiting the Wall, and set off for a brisk walk, trying to walk off the tiredness of the night.

It was a pleasant tiredness, and she walked on, secure in the knowledge that she could take a catnap in the afternoon, when her lodgings were quietest, then sleep all night, too—if she could. All too often her nights off were broken by dreams of Adam, of what might have been, and she knew she could not go on much longer. The fresh air helped, though, and she felt that, at last, she would sleep well and waken refreshed, even though the following day held nothing of any interest.

Then she remembered. She was lunching with David and Lynne Hanington tomorrow. It would be good to talk shop, to hear about the patients. She might, too, hear about Adam. She longed to know how he was getting along. She was aware that work on the house had begun again, because she had driven past only a couple of days before. So Sonia Kenlow had kept her word, and for that she was grateful.

She sank down on a grassy hillock, her eyes unseeing, her heart and mind with Adam, tramping across the Northumberland countryside, pausing to kiss her every now and again. She pulled herself together. It was only a dream. She had made the choice not to see him again, and the less time she spent dwelling on the matter the better. Instead she let her mind go blank, absorbing through her pores the glorious emptiness of Northumberland.

The sky was bluer than ever, decorated with small fluffy white clouds. To her right, green hills curved gently, while straight ahead was a coppice beside which the trackway ran. Idly she ran a hand along the top of the Wall. Here the Roman Wall was reasonably well preserved, though in other places it was no more than a pile of rubble, overgrown and neglected.

On a clear day it was possible to scan vast distances, and Isobel wished she knew more of the geography of the area. Yet it was enough to know that the Wall had been there nearly two thousand years and would be there long after she was gone.

At peace for once, she turned and was about to

retrace her steps. Then she became aware of the watcher, and a prickle of fear disturbed her new-found tranquillity.

'Adam!' The glad cry broke from her before she could use her brain. It was tired from the long hours on duty and not functioning efficiently. Remembering that she must not give Sonia Kenlow cause for jealousy, she remained where she was instead of running to meet him.

'I saw your car as I was on my way to the coast,' he explained, as he scrambled over some rubble, and Isobel smiled politely, wondering why he was going to the coast but unwilling to ask. He paused once he was beside her, and she trembled, afraid he would touch her. She knew that she no longer had the strength to resist him.

He stood stiffly, his face cold and set . . . 'Why did you tell June you were heading for the coast?' he asked, his voice as cold as his face.

'It was the truth, that's why,' she replied simply. 'I thought about going to that . . .' She stopped, not wanting him to know she yearned to revisit the fishing village. 'I thought the coast might be crowded, so I changed my mind about going,' she hastened on. 'It's only my second visit to Hadrian's Wall and I decided a brisk walk might help me to sleep. I'm on nights,' she explained, and Adam nodded curtly.

'The Home is going ahead full steam,' he said into the lengthening silence.

'I'm pleased. When will you take the first patients?' Here at least was neutral territory. They could talk shop without arguing.

But it seemed they could not. 'I didn't think you

were interested!' he barked, startling her.

'Well, of course I am!' she protested. 'That's why I was so upset because the work was stopped!' He must know about the stoppage by now, so she wasn't telling tales behind Sonia's back.

He frowned. 'I didn't realise you knew. It was only one day.'

Isobel brightened. 'I'm glad! I thought she . . . they might stop for . . .'

'She?' he queried.

'The workmen. They weren't there when I passed one day and I . . .'

'Presumed that Sonia had paid them off?' he broke in, and she nodded.

'Not so. They were on strike over some little matter—an unofficial strike. It was just the one day,' he explained, watching her closely as the swift tide of colour came and went in her face, leaving her paler than before, the smattering of freckles more noticeable.

Gently Adam cupped her small face in his hands, and a tremor shot through her. 'June Bland and I put two and two together after you left so hurriedly. Sonia supplied the rest of the answers,' he went on grimly. 'I had already decided to break off my engagement. It wasn't fair to Sonia, to you *or* to me. It was unfair to the patients and staff as well,' he smiled wryly, dropping a kiss on her pert nose. 'I've been miserable without you, Bella.'

'Have you?' she murmured, lifting her face for his kiss, her eyes wide with happiness.

'Mm, very miserable.'

Isobel drew back, remembering the Home for the disabled, Adam's pride and joy. 'Your Home,

Adam! The Home you wanted. I . . . they were still working there last week!'

'June found the necessary money,' he told her. 'Some of her own and some from her pet doctor! He's going to provide a certain amount of medical cover for the patients, if required.'

'Did Sonia withdraw her support? Was that why . . .' she began, guilt creeping over her.

'I broke off the engagement, as I said. Gradually I got part of the story out of Sonia. I'd already bought the house from her, so she couldn't stop the work. It was an idle threat. Then June offered the money so that I could pay for the alterations. Before then I decided that *my* personal happiness came before anyone else's. In those circumstances, it wouldn't have been fair to marry Sonia. I suppose it isn't fair to marry you either, but I intend to!'

His kiss was wholly satisfying, and when she could struggle free she grinned up at him, her proud, arrogant northerner. 'Why isn't it fair to marry me, sir?'

A smile lit up his normally cold, autocratic face. 'You're too young for me, pet. I've always thought so. *And* you're a southerner!'

Isobel stood on tiptoe to kiss the cleft in his chin, her heart bursting with happiness. Then her face fell. 'You do understand about Paul and me, don't you? There was never anything . . .'

Adam's lips silenced her. 'I know, Bella,' he said softly.

Once he had released her she half wondered if she should mention Paul's diagnosis of her, one that was branded upon her soul. Yet this was Adam, not Paul. His eyes caressed her, heating her heart and body, and she felt anything but frigid! Perhaps later she might confess and they would laugh about it together, on their honeymoon. Paul was so very, very wrong! 'I'll try to love, honour and obey you, even if I *am* a southerner!' she whispered, her heart glowing.

'You'd better!' he warned, gathering her into the warm safety of his arms again. 'I'll beat you every time you're disobedient! Even yon Hadrian couldn't keep down the wild northerners!'

They stood by the ancient Wall, locked in their own little world of love, while the sun smiled down at them. Isobel liked to think that Hadrian, too, gave them his blessing.

Mills & Boon

4 Doctor Nurse Romances
FREE

Coping with the daily tragedies and ordeals of a busy hospital, and sharing the satisfaction of a difficult job well done, people find themselves unexpectedly drawn together. Mills & Boon Doctor Nurse Romances capture perfectly the excitement, the intrigue and the emotions of modern medicine, that so often lead to overwhelming and blissful love. By becoming a regular reader of Mills & Boon Doctor Nurse Romances you can enjoy SIX superb new titles every two months plus a whole range of special benefits: your very own personal membership card, a free newsletter packed with recipes, competitions, bargain book offers, plus big cash savings.

AND an Introductory FREE GIFT for YOU.
Turn over the page for details.

**Fill in and send this coupon back today
and we'll send you**
4 Introductory
Doctor Nurse Romances yours to keep
FREE

At the same time we will reserve a
subscription to Mills & Boon
Doctor Nurse Romances for you. Every
two months you will receive the latest
6 new titles, delivered direct to your door.
You don't pay extra for delivery. Postage and
packing is always completely Free.
There is no obligation or commitment –
you receive books only for
as long as you want to.

**It's easy! Fill in the coupon below and return it to
MILLS & BOON READER SERVICE, FREEPOST, P.O. BOX 236,
CROYDON, SURREY CR9 9EL.**

**Please note: READERS IN SOUTH AFRICA write to
Mills & Boon Ltd., Postbag X3010,
Randburg 2125, S. Africa.**

- -

FREE BOOKS CERTIFICATE

**To: Mills & Boon Reader Service, FREEPOST, P.O. Box 236,
Croydon, Surrey CR9 9EL.**

Please send me, free and without obligation, four Dr. Nurse Romances, and reserve a Reader
Service Subscription for me. If I decide to subscribe I shall receive, following my free parcel of
books, six new Dr. Nurse Romances every two months for £6.00*, post and packing free. If I
decide not to subscribe, I shall write to you within 10 days. The free books are mine to keep in
any case. I understand that I may cancel my subscription at any time simply by writing to you. I
am over 18 years of age.
Please write in BLOCK CAPITALS.

Name _____

Address _____

_____

_____ Postcode _____

SEND NO MONEY — TAKE NO RISKS

Remember, postcodes speed delivery. Offer applies in UK only and is not valid to present subscribers. Mills &
Boon reserve the right to exercise discretion in granting membership. If price changes are

8DN changes are necessary you will be notified. Offer expires 31st March 1986.

EP15R

* Subject to possible V.A.T.